STREET

A CHARLIE STREET Crime Thriller

STREET is Book 1,
the introduction to the
STREET LAW series

LINDA STYLE

PRAISE FOR LINDA'S NOVELS
Winner of the Daphne du Maurier Award
Winner of the Orange Rose Award
Holt Medallion Award of Merit
***USA TODAY* Best Romance of 2012 List**

"Linda Style writes an **intriguing, fast-moving, intelligent story**. I'll be on the lookout for more."
~Linda Lael Miller, NY Times & *USA Today* bestselling author

"**STREET knocked my socks off.** Crime fighting has never been so sexy and so satisfying."
~Fire Fiction Reviews

"**Wow. This story really takes off**. STREET grabs you from the start and never lets go." ~Author review

"**Linda Style's DETROIT RULES is a brilliant crime thriller** with a gutsy, streetwise heroine! Mystery, danger, seduction, and action, this big novel has it all!
~Eve Paludan, national bestselling author.

"**Trust Linda Style to always offer a fascinating story** and DETROIT RULES is no exception."
~Amazon review

"**Fast-paced action, high emotion** and many surprises along the way. I love Linda Style novels and DETROIT RULES may be my favorite book she's written."
~Amazon review

"**Absolutely spellbinding**. A great plot…extraordinary in every way." ~*Coffee Time Reviews*

"A tale of striking intensity…a compelling romance. Style has a gift for creating intriguing settings and characterizations …escape to a world of danger, intrigue and passion. A compelling romance."
~Cindy Penn, *Midwest Book Review*

"An exhilarating romantic suspense that keeps readers wondering until the end. Action-packed…a strong intrigue." ~Harriet Klausner, *The Best Reviews*

"…**Style writes with style**… Style writes highly original stories that include characters with great depth. An exciting, heart-stopping reading experience you won't want to miss. It proves once again, Ms. Style writes with style." ~Suzanne Tucker, *Old Book Barn Gazette*

"A riveting read that will leave readers glued to the pages. Ms. Style has a flair for suspense. A series you won't want to miss. ~*Romance Designs*

"Tense, suspenseful and full of surprises. The pages seem to turn by themselves. When a story engages my mind as well as my emotions, I know I'm hooked."
~*The Romance Reader*

"Great Story! So intense, with strong feelings of love and betrayal. Mystery and danger…another couldn't put it down story you'll really love."
~*Rendezvous Magazine*

"Brilliantly creative, an engrossing read of romance and suspense…strong characters and a beguiling plot."
~Donna Zapf, *Cataromance*

STREET

A CHARLIE STREET Crime Thriller

**STREET is Book 1,
the introduction to the
STREET LAW series**

LINDA STYLE

LMS PRESS
Gilbert, Arizona

LMSPress@cox.net

STREET
Copyright © 2019 by Linda Style
LMS Press
Gilbert, AZ 85234
LMSPress@cox.net
All Rights Reserved

Except for use in any review, the reproduction or utilization of this work in whole or in part in any form by any electronic, mechanical or other means, now known or hereafter invented, including xerography, photocopying and recording, or in any information storage or retrieval system, is forbidden without the written permission of the author.

Copyright infringement is against the law.
All characters in this book have no existence outside the imagination of the author and have no relation whatsoever to anyone bearing the same name or names. They are not even distantly inspired by any individual known or unknown to the author, and all incidents are pure invention. Some parts of this book have been used in a short story in the past, and some facts have been subject to artistic license.

ISBN: 9781726771580

1st Edition -- ALL RIGHTS RESERVED

Cover Designer: Rogenna Brewer
sweettoheat.blogspot.com

Copy Editor: Eve Paluden

Formatting: Nina Pierce of Seaside Publications
ninapierce.com/book-formatting

ACKNOWLEDGMENTS

My deep appreciation to my dear friends who have been with me on this journey almost from the beginning and are always available to offer helpful advice or simply be my sounding board as I go through the process of writing each book.
Thank you so much
Ann Voss Peterson, Susan Vaughan,
Ginny Vail, and Sheila Seabrook.

And, as always, my love and thanks
to my beautiful family.

CHAPTER ONE

Detroit, Michigan
A while ago…

PLEASE, PLEASE, PLEASE. I'll do anything, Charlie Street promised whatever god, spirit, or the devil himself, if he could produce the means to save her.

The man across the table hid behind dark Ray-Bans and a charcoal gray hoodie, pulled so close around his face all she could see was his hooked nose sticking out.

The others were dressed in personality statements of their own—a neon orange T-shirt and hair spiked like a rhino, a dude who looked like he should be auditioning for a role on *Empire*, and a guy sporting a polyester leisure suit from the '70s, complete with mutton chops. All typical garb at a Texas Hold'em table on Saturday night at the Greektown Casino.

Charlie wore her usual. Black. Tonight it was a dress. Low-cut, short, and sexy. With five-inch red stilettos. Anything to distract.

And it looked like her ploy might've worked.

The game was down to her and Hoodie.

If she won, the money would literally save her life.

Her nerves tensed. Next up…the turn card.

She studied her opponent. Stone still. No tells.

A shuffling sound came from behind her. Body heat. Some idiot looking over her shoulder. Breaking her concentration.

The dealer turned a seven of hearts, giving her two options. Adrenaline rushed as she calculated the odds. On the table, the seven of hearts, a Jack of spades, a two of hearts and an Ace. Not even a pair. Hoodie hadn't been betting. And with the odd cards on the table, if he had anything at all he'd be shoving in the chips.

She had an open ended straight, seven high, and four hearts. Three ways to go. A straight or a flush. One card left.

She swallowed, laid a hand on her chips. "All in."

Her heart pounding a hole in her chest, she pushed what was left of her winnings forward. If Hoodie met her bet and she won, she'd rake in over fifty K. If he didn't see her bet, she'd win and still have enough to make the move she'd been working toward since she left law school.

Hoodie fingered his chips, making little *clickity click* sounds, stared at the cards, then at her. Maybe. Other than the lift of his chin, it was hard to know. But he'd be looking for tells, too, to see if she might be bluffing. Which at this point, she was. But the odds were in her favor three different ways.

He shoved in the rest of his chips.

Her heart raced. Sweat broke under her arms. One card—give her a three, an eight, or a heart. She had this!

They flipped over their cards. Hoodie had a potential straight…inside.

Damn! Not the eight. It would give him a higher straight.

Okay. A three or a heart. The percentages were still on her side.

The room hummed with anticipation.

She launched to her feet.

The dealer flipped the last card. The river.

She stared. Blood drained from her limbs. No. That. Could. Not. Happen. No, no, no.

Her throat closed. She gulped for air.

She swung around and stumbled into the man standing behind her. Barely looking at him except to note he was much taller than she was, she shoved past him and tore through the crowd, tears suddenly streaming.

She'd lost it. Every penny of the money she'd saved for two years. Her brain stalled. She couldn't think as she pushed through a blurry sea of people.

How could it…how could she…be so stupid?

Blindly charging through the game rooms on her way to the parking garage, bile rose in her throat. She passed a restroom, backed up and stumbled inside. Unable to make it to the toilet, she hit the sink, leaned over, and puked her guts out.

Arms on the sink, she ran the water, cupped her hands to collect enough to rinse, and spit… three times.

Seeing herself in the mirror, she laughed, her voice a high cackle. Mascara ran down her cheeks and ringed her eyes. All she needed was some big red lips and she'd look like a clown. A very sad clown. An idiot clown.

Only an idiot would've made that last play. One more bet to see if he'd stay and raise. That's what she should've done. She'd lost focus. The guy behind had unnerved her, and she'd jumped the gun. Stupid. But the most stupid part was that she was there in the first place.

Pulling a tissue from her purse, a dollar bill fluttered to the floor.

She stared at it, then laughed, tearing up at the same time. Well—she hauled in a lungful of air—she wasn't totally broke.

The irony was that she'd done just the opposite of what she'd started out to do earlier in the evening. Now instead of having enough money to quit her job and work for herself, she'd have to work a long time at Reston, Barrett and Brown just to get back what she'd lost.

If she didn't kill herself first. Working for a law firm that had no conscience was akin to selling her soul.

On her way to the garage, passing several rows of quarter slots lined up like robots, she spotted a Megabucks slot on the end. She fingered the dollar, the only thing between her and poverty.

When she was little, her dad had given her a toy bank shaped like a slot machine and every time she put in a penny, the wheels would spin and lights would flash.

It was an omen of some kind, wasn't it? Her dad looking over her from above.

She stopped and not bothering to sit, shoved in the money, pushed the button and watched the reels spin. A Megabucks icon bounced to a stop. The teaser. Then another…and another.

Bells rang, lights flashed, red, blue, green, and yellow. She might have screamed. The woman sitting on the stool next to her screamed. A gaggle of white-haired seniors with name tags on their shirts huddled around her as the sound and light show continued, the slot numbers spinning crazily to total up the win, finally stopping at twenty-five thousand, four hundred and forty-four dollars.

Charlie's eyes glazed over. Her heart pounded.

"Hit the button," a man's voice came from somewhere on her right. "Someone will come and take care of you. They need to get the information from the machine before any payout."

Charlie knew. This was not her first rodeo. Still, she was stunned. One minute she'd lost it all, and the next she'd won half back. Could she actually win that much on a dollar slot?

Apparently yes, she discovered when a casino employee came over, and a sometime later, she'd cashed out. Her blood rushed. She should play more, win more. A gambler's mantra.

The smart thing to do, though, would be to leave. But...when a machine was hot, chances were it would hit again. Or maybe a different slot. Wheel of Fortune. Progressive games paid the most, didn't they?

Unbelievable. She'd gone from the lowest of lows to reclaiming her life, all in the space of a few minutes. Her nerves tingled. Her pulse raced. If she stuck around, she could break even. Get it all back...and more.

The adrenaline rush of a win pulled at her, lured her back to the slot. Seeing someone at the machine, a mix of disappointment and relief shot through her. Another omen. Half of her nest egg was better than nothing...and, no, she wasn't going to tempt fate one more second.

Charlie hadn't been to the casino in two years, not since her family conspired and subjected her to their version of an intervention. She shouldn't be here now, and if she stuck around long enough…

Pulling away before she changed her mind, she charged through the casino doors leading to the attached parking garage. Her car was on the same floor at the end of the second row. Once there she would be safe from herself.

The heat of an uncharacteristically warm October mixed with noxious gas fumes trapped in the parking garage made her stomach roil again. She got out her keys and aimed the fob. Just as she clicked the UNLOCK button something bumped her from behind. Hard. Her purse yanked from her fingers.

"No!" Charlie grasped the strap...and stared into the cold eyes of a man wearing a black beanie. He swatted at her and yanked again. She clutched even harder and screamed. No petty thief was going to ruin the rest of her life.

"Let go, bitch." Grappling over the purse, the man shouldered her into the wall, hitting and jabbing with his free hand.

"No way, asshole!" Charlie held so tight her nails dug into her palms. She screamed at the top of her lungs and butted him with her head. So much for her self-defense training.

"Crazy bitch." Another guy ran over. Burly, twice her size. "Let go, or I'll fucking kill you," he spat out and punched her in the face.

Stars flashed before her eyes. She tightened her grip. *Her money. She couldn't lose her money.*

The bigger guy pressed her face against the wall with one hand, his other went around her neck. Tightening…choking…her screams a strangled gurgle. Light and dark faded in and out. Vision blurring. She felt the purse strap scraping across her fingers as she lost her grip.

Voices…shouting, yelling. "*Ladrón estúpido.*" A man's voice.

More scuffling, shoving, a flurry of arms and fists, and then the pressure around her neck fell away, and a blurry form came into focus. Familiar. The man she'd nearly run over and shoved away when leaving the poker table. He leveled his gaze at her attacker and hissed, "You should never hit a woman, *cabrón*."

Charlie's vision cleared enough see her savior throw a kick that sent the thief across the hood of a car five feet away. Someone's arms came under hers from behind, holding her up, but her knees wobbled, unsteady. Dizzy...

"He scared them away!" A woman's voice. "But they got your purse."

A buzz filled Charlie's ears.
And then the concrete came up to meet her.

CHAPTER TWO

"THEY SAY HE killed his wife."

"Was that before or after he swindled the taxpayers and misappropriated state funds?" Charlie teased the receptionist whose muffled voice announced her client was waiting.

The woman laughed. As much as Charlie hated working for Reston, Barrett and Brown, the largest and most prestigious law firm in Detroit, she'd made a couple of good friends at the firm and would truly miss them when she left.

Except now she'd have to stay even longer than planned. Her penance for stupidly losing all her money. It wasn't her fault she was assaulted and robbed, but she had only herself to blame for going to the casino in the first place.

"I'll be right there."

Charlie had heard all the gossip and rumors about her new client, Senator Alvin Hawker, and had dismissed them. It was hard not to feel sympathy for a man whose seven-year-old son had been abducted and, after nearly a year without a word—not even a ransom request—there was little hope the boy was still alive.

As politicians went, Senator Hawker was the only one around who seemed sincere and had done several things to fix some of the inner-city problems. Despite all the rumors planted by his opponents, already gearing up for the next election, she believed in him.

And as his attorney, her job was to provide enough evidence to keep the senator from being indicted for misuse of state money, which he'd allegedly used to fund extravagant vacations and to support his friends. Including a former mistress. Pretty much business as usual in Detroit, but she didn't believe it.

From all that she'd read about the man, and from all he'd done since getting elected, he appeared to be an honest man. She'd cheered him on. For once, the people had elected a politician who was different. If given the support he needed, there was no telling how much he could accomplish. Senator Hawker could set the state on the right path again.

She went out to meet her client, as she usually did, rather than having someone bring him to her office. A more personal way to begin the relationship. As she got closer, she noticed another man standing just behind and to the side of the senator. Her stomach dropped.

He was the same man who'd rescued her last night. Shit. She'd planned to keep her ill-fated visit to the casino a secret.

"Senator Hawker." Charlie extended a hand. "Nice to meet you. I'm Charlize Street."

The senator was a tall man, with dull brown hair, graying at the temples. Distinguished, except the gray made him look older than he probably was. Late fifties. He sported a golf-course tan, and although he wasn't fat, she could tell he was soft and doughy under the designer suit.

"I know who you are, Ms. Street. And to be honest, I have to say I'm not entirely happy Douglas isn't doing this himself. But looking at your record, I was impressed. Your percentage of acquittals is to be admired." He gave her a wide, welcoming smile.

Douglas Reston was her boss, and it boosted her ego to know that maybe he really did think she was a better fit to be the lead on this case than he was.

She returned the wide smile. "Well, Senator, be assured I'm going to do everything I can to maintain those percentages." She glanced at the man next to him.

"Luc Cabrera, my security specialist," the senator said, motioning to the man standing behind him.

Meaning bodyguard. She extended a hand to Cabrera. So, had the senator been checking her out, and the man's fortuitous appearance at the casino wasn't random?

"Pleased to meet you, Mr. Cabrera."

Leaning to shake hands, she got a whiff of his cologne. *Armani Acqua di Gio.* Nice. His thumb trailed across the back of her hand.

"My pleasure, Ms. Street." He nodded, his dark-eyed gaze enveloping her, familiar, as if they shared some big secret. His slight accent made the simple repetition of her name a seductive overture. He was smooth. Very smooth.

Walking together into her office, the senator said, "I'm sure Douglas has stressed how anxious I am to get this cleared up as soon as possible."

"Of course. Mr. Reston will be working with me to do exactly that, Senator." And she was just as anxious as he was. The sooner she could get this case wrapped up, the better, so he could get back to doing his job and not waste time with manufactured scandals.

The senator sat in the client chair and Cabrera, wearing a black, well-tailored suit, silver gray shirt and a dark tie, stood by the door. Charlie motioned, indicating he should sit, too.

"He's fine where he is," the senator said. "Let's get this done."

After explaining the allegations and the charges they

might be up against, should it come to that, Charlie handed the senator a list of the records to which she'd need access. All routine, standard procedure.

Reading, the man nodded his agreement. "I'll have my secretary get everything to you within a few days. Everything except my personal business records."

Charlie studied the man. He clearly didn't understand. "Excuse me, Senator. We need everything on the list."

"I'd be happy to oblige, Ms. Street," he said, now looking directly at her. "But the records for that period of time no longer exist. My former assistant left the position over a year ago, and we haven't been able to locate the records since."

Charlie perused the senator's file on her computer monitor, scrolled down to his former assistant's information. "Mia Powers was your administrative assistant during the time in question. Are you saying she destroyed all your records?"

"I don't know. She took the computer with her and disappeared."

"Do you have any idea why?"

"I suspect it was because she knew I was going to let her go and hire someone else."

"My records show she also worked for you as a nanny to your son."

"Correct. After my wife died, I needed someone to be there and Mia was one of my most trusted employees. She volunteered and it worked out very well for a time. She was able to work from home a couple days a week and that really helped out with—" his voice hitched "—my son."

"I'm sorry. I hate to bring up a sensitive issue, but we have to be able to prove the opposite of what the state wants to prove. The records are critical. Have you tried to find Ms. Powers?"

"Of course. I hired the best investigator I could find.

But Mia seems to have vanished into thin air."

"We'll need the investigator's findings and even so, we'll also conduct our own search. If she can't be found, we need to show you did everything in your power to find her."

"From what I remember of the law, the burden of proof is on the prosecution, not the defense."

She steepled her hands. "Then I'm sure you also remember that while that's true, we still need to provide an airtight defense."

He sat back, grinned. "If I could do that, Ms. Street, I wouldn't be here, now would I?"

From what she'd researched, Hawker was an attorney, but had never practiced law. Not one day. He'd gone straight from law school into public service. But he was her client and despite all the flack he was getting from the press, she really did believe he was innocent. She smiled in return. "Right. And like I said, I'm going to do everything in my power to provide the best defense possible."

The man shifted in his chair, clenched his hands. "Good. I'm paying this firm a great deal of money to make this go away quickly," he said. "The longer it hangs on, the worse it looks on my resume, if you know what I mean." He winked at her.

She did know. It wouldn't be good for his chances of getting reelected.

"If you use the findings we already have things should move swiftly." He launched to his feet, his expression suddenly thoughtful. "Excuse me. I must to talk to Douglas for a moment." He swung around and loped toward the door. She got up and followed, but he was gone before she could spit out another word, leaving her and Cabrera staring at each other.

She cleared her throat. "You left last night before I had a chance to thank you."

"It is unnecessary."

"Why? Because you were spying on me?"

A slow smile tipped his lips. "Spying is such a crass word. I was enjoying watching a beautiful woman play a killer game of poker. You are very good, *bonita.*"

Bonita? She stiffened at the familiarity. "I don't know your motives, Mr. Cabrera, but it's hard to believe you just happened to be there watching me."

"It is the truth. I, too, excel at the game of poker, and I admired your skill so much I could not tear myself away."

"Are you saying you weren't there checking on me for the senator?"

"I can guarantee that was not why I was there. Although spying on you is a job I think I would like very much."

"So why didn't you tell the senator you saw me there?" If Cabrera had blabbed, the senator would have mentioned it for sure.

"I suspect for the same reason you did not report the robbery to the police."

She squelched a smile. The man was quick. Smart.

"I doubt our reasons are the same, however, I thank you again. You scared off those men and I'm grateful.

He nodded. "I'm sorry I was not able to retrieve your money."

Not as sorry as she was. Early this morning she'd had to contact her bank and credit card companies to stop any charges and get new cards. And she'd had to apply for a duplicate driver's license. "Thank you. I'm afraid it's gone for good."

"I am curious. Why did you fight with them? That can be a dangerous thing to do."

Charlie sighed. "I agree, it wasn't the wisest idea in the world. I guess I need to brush up on my self-defense skills."

"I would be happy to teach you. I have expert skills in martial arts as well."

"And you're modest, too."

But she didn't doubt his statement. The punch or kick she'd seen him throw had sent her assailant across the parking garage. She pulled her gaze from his. "You are a persistent man, Mr. Cabrera."

"Please, call me Lucas. Or Luc as my friends do."

"Okay...Luc." She looked him in the eyes again. "Let me be clear. While I'm grateful for your help last night, your boss is my client. You and I will not have any contact other than what's necessary to my work with the senator, and even then, it will be as little as possible. I'd appreciate it if we can leave it right there."

"As the lady wishes." He raised his hands.

The senator returned, stood behind Cabrera. "I spoke with Douglas. He will catch you up on our conversation. If you have any other questions about records and paperwork, please contact my administrative assistant."

Hands again clasped in front of him, Cabrera shifted his gaze from Charlie to the senator then to Charlie, again.

"Or you can get in touch with Luc." Senator Hawker motioned to the bodyguard, who produced a card from his pocket, and handed it to her, his fingers touching hers...lingering too long.

Oh, man. Was this guy full of himself or what? Dangerous came to mind. Hot. She took the card. LUCAS CABRERA, SECURITY SPECIALIST. A phone number was listed, and an email address. Nothing else.

"Thank you," she said, although she couldn't think of a single reason she'd have to call the bodyguard.

Cabrera grinned. Sexy. Masculine. Totally not her type. Although her father was half Mexican, her experiences with macho Latino men hadn't been stellar. Actually most men she'd been involved with fit that category.

Her father had been an exception, a strong supporter of equality for all. He'd had to be. He would never have gotten even close to her mother otherwise. From the time Charlie could remember, her father had told her she could do anything...be anything she wanted. And she'd believed him.

The senator was already walking down the hall to leave, so she moved to within inches of Cabrera, his body heat like fire scorching her skin. "Can you keep a secret?" she said, her voice low.

He moved even closer, his mouth nearly touching hers, his eagerness radiating. "Of course."

"Well, just between you and me, Luc..." she paused, moistened her lips "... I think you're a player, and you don't get to play with me."

Face to face, a long moment passed. Her nerves skittered.

Then he reached up, brushed his fingertips down her cheek. "I hear the words, *bonita*. But why do I not believe you?"

CHAPTER THREE

LUC WAITED BY the door for the senator to finish his phone call and tell Luc why he'd been summoned. He'd been working for the egotistical *cabrón* for three months now, preparing for the moment when his well-laid trap would come to fruition.

Doing the senator's grunt work was an inconvenience. As his bodyguard, Luc was on call for the senator, but he had plenty of time when not working to pursue other interests and activities. He could even manage another job, if it was brief.

But he wasn't going to do anything he couldn't quit in the middle. It was important to be available to the senator on a moment's notice.

He'd learned those times were when the senator's business was not related to the betterment of the state, but to the betterment of the senator's very large offshore bank account, and those times often involved people a senator wouldn't normally do business with.

Finally, after a lengthy call, the senator finished and turned to Luc. "The vice president and I were talking about our upcoming hunting trip in two weeks, and I want to make sure you're available."

"I am at your service, Senator Hawker."

"Good. Because I have something else I'd like you to do in the meantime. It involves my attorney on this fucking stupid misuse of state funds thing."

Luc's spirits lifted. Anything that put him in the proximity of the lovely Charlize Street was a most wonderful thing.

"I want you to keep a watch on Ms. Street, and if she uncovers anything related to Mia Powers and the records that bitch whore stole from me, I want to know about it."

The skin on his neck prickled. Luc clenched his hand into a fist. *Restricción, Nico.* Restraint. The time will come. It wasn't the first time the senator's disrespect for the fairer sex had Luc seconds from ending him. But Luc's goal was far more important. Maybe when his job was completed, he'd do the women of the world a favor and dispose of the entitled *misógino,* too.

"Watching the woman will be easy. But finding out what she knows may be more difficult." His research showed she was an excellent attorney. Honest. She wasn't going to be talking about anything to him, even if the senator gave the go-ahead. She'd said as much.

"I have every confidence you can figure out a way, Luc. I saw how she looked at you."

"Looks can be deceiving, Senator. And I am a mere bodyguard, not a spy."

"I will increase the amount on your contract."

"It is unnecessary, Senator. You already pay me very well."

The senator looked at Luc from under his brows. "And I will ensure you meet my friend, Vice President Spector. I believe you two have much in common."

Luc caught himself a fraction of a second before his head snapped up.

"You two being from the same state, and all," the senator continued. "He did a lot for your people when he was a senator there."

Oh, yes, the former senator from Arizona did do a

lot for *his people*. Luc knew first-hand. "My apologies that I am too busy to pay much attention to politics."

Hawker snorted. "Just as well. Too many people think they know what's going on and vote idiots into office."

Luc smiled and nodded. It was one thing on which they could agree. Senator Hawker and Vice President Spector being prime examples. The righteous Senator Hawker would be very surprised when he learned the truth about his good friend Spector on their little hunting trip.

Luc had no need for cruelty or vengeance. But in the Vice President's case, he would allow a little self-indulgence.

"So, we're good then," Hawker said, his crisp tone ending the subject of money. "Find a way to keep tabs on the pretty little attorney and we won't have to think about her having an accident."

Luc had other ideas for the pretty little attorney. Keeping tabs on her would be a soothing balm for his black soul.

He loved women. They were his Achilles' heel. And the sexy attorney with mad poker-playing skills was like a blossoming flower, her sweet petals begging to be plucked. Beauty and brains. The ultimate turn-on.

He'd be happy to seduce her if necessary, and he might do it anyway. Sometimes he just couldn't help himself. But he would have no qualms about killing her if she got in his way.

Working for the senator was the perfect cover for the job he had waited years to complete and in two weeks, it would be mission accomplished. If the corrupt senator got in his way, he'd take him out too.

Trained as an assassin, Luc knew how to kill a man in almost every possible way, but his most expert skills were in long and short-range weapons and hand-to-hand combat. He was an expert in computer hacking and spoke seven different languages. He could play with the best of them. Vice President Spector, even with the secret service at his side, wouldn't have a chance.

The politicians' annual hunting trip was the perfect place for the vice president to have an accident. All Luc had to do was wait. And keep the pretty little attorney from messing up his plans.

"Hey, Max." Charlie had talked to Max Scofield very little since she'd worked as a public defender and had used him to investigate a few cases for her. As a private investigator, he could do things she couldn't as an attorney for the county. Max was experienced, fast, and good at keeping a low profile.

Most of all, she trusted him. Something that didn't happen often with most of the men she met these days. "How free are you? I have a job if you're available."

"Anything for you, sweetheart."

They made arrangements for lunch, and two hours later she and Max were sitting at the American Coney Island Restaurant on Lafayette Boulevard laughing over Coney dogs and chili-cheese fries. The spicy scent of chili and hot dogs brought fond memories for Charlie. Her first time there had been with her dad, and she'd been a fan ever since. Working nearby she ate at the iconic restaurant, which had been doing business in downtown Detroit for over eighty years, several times every month

"So, what's up?" Max asked. "I thought you were going to open your own firm and take me with you."

"There's been a slight glitch. I need to work for Douglas a while longer. But the plan to do that is still in place, and I promise there will be a spot for you at

Street Law. But right now, I need to find someone. A woman named Mia Powers, former assistant to Senator Hawker."

"Wasn't there some scandal about Powers being the senator's mistress?"

Max had a great memory, a useful asset for a P.I. "Not my concern." She shifted her sitting position in the fifties-style chrome chair to keep the sun from her eyes.

Max ran his knuckles over the two-day growth on his chin. "Rumor has it, he killed his wife."

"Rumor has a lot of things that aren't true."

His brows lifted. "You know different? Maybe his mistress helped kill his wife, and he got rid of the mistress, too."

It was no secret the senator was having an affair with his assistant, Mia, when his wife died. It was no secret he'd moved said assistant into his home within two weeks after his wife's death from drowning in the bathtub after overdosing on pills and booze.

"No, I don't know different, but there's never been an investigation or any evidence to suggest his wife's death was anything but an accident. It's pure speculation. A slow news day."

"Sometimes there's a kernel of truth in rumors."

"Well, I'm not into conspiracy theories and until there's evidence to the contrary, the man is innocent until proven guilty." Not to mention she really wanted to believe he was innocent of the charges. The senator had done so much good for the state, it was hard to believe he was corrupt. He wasn't the most pleasant man to work with, but that had nothing to do with the job she was paid to do.

She took a breath. As Hawker's attorney, her job was to represent him and defend him if necessary. Which meant finding the information to prevent a grand jury indictment. "I'll see what police records I can get. I know someone who might be able to help." She knew a few people, including the assistant AG, Alan Chenowith. They'd dated in college, seriously for a while. "Regardless, I need to find Mia Powers. Can you do some digging?"

"Sure."

She gave him the packet of information she'd prepared. "I have an appointment with Esther Powers, Mia's mother, later today, so you can cross it off your—"

"Don't look now," Max said, indicating something behind her with his eyes. "There's a man watching us. On your left, three tables behind."

Two rows of tables lined the windows on each side in the restaurant about seven feet apart and another shorter row in the middle, and she couldn't look without being obvious. "What does he look like?"

"Thirties. Dark hair, looks tall, athletic build, one seventyish, dark suit, white shirt. Looks like a young Antonio Banderas, but not as pretty."

Hot blood rushed through her veins. "Unfuckingbelievable."

"Someone you know?" Max smiled and waggled his eyebrows.

"Unfortunately. He works for the senator."

"And?"

"The senator's bodyguard." Her first instinct was to get up and confront Cabrera. But that would give him enormous satisfaction. Instead, she jotted down a note on a napkin and folded it in half. When the waiter came around, she asked him to please deliver it to Cabrera's table.

"Since when do senators need bodyguards?"

"I don't know. Maybe Hawker had some death threats." Even when false, a rumor always got legs when politicians were involved. Mismanaging state funds could make a lot of people angry. Who knew what kooks might come out of the woodwork?

"Okay. What's the bodyguard's problem?"

She shrugged. "It doesn't matter. Ignore him." She realized then that while it was a bit strange for the senator to have need for a bodyguard, something else seemed off. Something about Luc. "He's probably just having lunch."

She reached in her purse and took out her lipstick mirror. Holding it up, at first she saw only the black and white checkerboard pattern on the floor, but changing position, she spotted him, watched as he opened the napkin. After a moment, he looked up and smiled. Sexy. Inviting. Even from this far away she could see his eyes twinkle. Then he kissed the napkin, put it in his breast pocket, got up, and left the restaurant.

Her pulse raced.

"You're blushing."

"Hot flash."

Max chuckled. "Yeah, in twenty years, maybe. But, hey, I gotta give the guy kudos. Whoever he is, he's done the impossible."

"What's that?"

"Got you flustered."

"If I'm flustered, it's because I'm pissed. The bozo has been following me."

"Really? Why would the senator's bodyguard be following you?"

"That's what I want to know."

"What did you write on the napkin?"

Heat filled her chest thinking about Luc's response, the way he'd kissed the napkin.

"I told him to fuck off."

Max laughed, again. "I don't think he got the message."

CHAPTER FOUR

CHARLIE CHECKED THE address again. Mia Powers' mother lived in Grosse Pointe, one of the elite 'burbs of Detroit. The old brick Colonial on Touraine Road between Kercheval Avenue and Grosse Pointe Boulevard in Grosse Pointe Farms, a subdivision on Lake St. Clair, had a four-car garage larger than the house in Corktown where Charlie had grown up.

She pulled into the curved drive and got out, marveling at how different the landscape could be only a few miles from the blight that lay on the other side of Alter Road, the symbolic dividing line between wealth and poverty. Her old Ford Focus was definitely out of place in this driveway.

Hurrying to the door, the chill wind whipped her long scarf into her face and her hair into her eyes. A gardener, in front of the next house down, struggled to rake leaves into a contained pile. The smell of crisp, dry leaves assaulted her nostrils, reminding her how she and Landon used to jump into the piles of leaves her dad had raked. They'd thought it great fun, until he'd made them clean up their mess.

A lifetime ago. Before her dad had gone to jail. Before he'd been murdered.

After years of hunting for her father's killer and being forced to resign her job with the Wayne County

Public Defender's Office because of it, she'd stopped her search. She'd had to. Doing anything outside of what her job entailed at RB&B could get her fired. She couldn't risk that again.

But the most important thing she'd learned within hours of starting the job at RB&B was that she had to tread very carefully when working with particular clients who had her bosses by the short hairs.

RB&B's business relied on wealthy people in powerful positions. And at the moment, her livelihood depended on her employer. A sellout? Yes. Every second of every day was pure torture. She filled her lungs with air. *It's temporary*. That was her mantra for however long it took to save enough money to leave and start her own firm.

Although she was fifteen minutes early for the appointment with Mrs. Powers, she rang the bell. Within seconds, the front door swung open, and a woman about Charlie's mother's age stood in the doorway. She was an elegant blonde, with the kind of bearing that suggested money, private schools, and a long, important family lineage. "Mrs. Powers?"

"Yes. And you're Charlie Street." She produced a smile on cue and extended a hand.

"I am," Charlie said, returning the smile and shaking the woman's hand. Extra points to the woman for not spouting the usual, 'I thought you'd be a man.'

"Do come in." Mrs. Powers motioned Charlie into the two-story foyer, past a curved staircase to a room on her left, small like an old-fashioned parlor. "Can I take your jacket?"

"Thanks, but I'm good." The place felt like a refrigerator and wearing only her usual black blazer over a white knit tank, she'd freeze her ass off without the jacket.

Mrs. Powers motioned for Charlie to sit on an

antique settee that looked like it could withstand about fifty pounds at the most.

"My mother loves antiques," Charlie said, an attempt to put the woman at ease.

"How lovely. So many people destroy the old in favor of the new. I think it's a shame."

"I agree." Okay, small talk over. She cleared her throat. "As I mentioned, I'm representing Senator Hawker and, since your daughter worked for him for a time, I'm hoping you can give me some information."

"I have to admit, I was surprised when your assistant made the appointment. I really don't have any good feelings about the senator after what he did to my daughter."

Charlie leaned forward. "Do you mean because he was going to let her go from the job?"

The woman's eyes widened. "Oh, no. I don't think Mia knew. She never said anything to me. She was very happy with the job. She loved everything about it. She loved Zack. She would have been heartbroken if the senator let her go. No, what I meant was how the senator treated her. He's a very mean man. He took advantage of her. And she so adored him, she'd have done anything for him."

A mean man. Really? "How was he mean?"

"Mia didn't say a lot, but the last time I saw her she had bruises. She wouldn't tell me how she got them." She closed her eyes for a moment. "But I knew."

"When was that?"

"Well, it was our thirtieth anniversary, which was a year and a half ago."

"Do you think she left because he abused her?" Hard to imagine, but Charlie had worked with several victims of abuse; money and status had nothing to do with it. Abuse crossed all lines of ethnicity and social status. Many dark secrets lurked behind elegant closed doors.

"No. She loved that little boy. She would have stayed no matter what. She would have said something if she were planning to go away."

"Did you see her often?"

Powers shook her head, eyes darkening. "No, I didn't see her a lot when she was working for the senator, but she came to dinner on the holidays. And she called." She shook her head again. "That's why I'm certain something is horribly wrong. She hasn't contacted me or anyone in all this time. That's not normal for Mia."

"So you don't think she was angry because she was going to be fired from the job?"

"I think the senator makes it sound like that's what happened, and the police believe him. I filed a missing persons' report, but they as much as told me they weren't going to do anything."

"Because?"

"They said an adult person has a right to leave home and live wherever they wish, however they wish. And given the senator's statements about how she threatened to leave when he told her he didn't want her to work for him anymore, the authorities did very little."

"Do you know anything about her personal relationship with Senator Hawker?"

"No. Mia never talked about that. She kept those kinds of things to herself."

"And you haven't talked to her since she left?"

Mrs. Powers shook her head. Tears welled in her eyes. "Everything changed when she went to work for the senator. It was like she became a different person."

"What kind of work did she do for the senator before switching to the new job with him?"

"I don't know exactly. She said it was classified, and she couldn't talk about it, but she made very good money."

"Did she have friends? A roommate?"

"I only knew her college friends. After college, she kept to herself. We saw her on holidays and special occasions, but she never invited us to visit her."

"The address I have for her before going to work for the senator was in Troy," Charlie said.

"Troy. Yes, but she moved from there. She did have a roommate. I can't think of her name, but I have it somewhere. I can look it up."

Mrs. Powers got up and left the room. When she returned, she handed Charlie a piece of paper with the name Bunny written on it and an address.

"I'm afraid I don't know any more than I told you. I wish I did. I wish I'd paid more attention."

Charlie had heard that same regret more times than she could count in the five years she'd been practicing law—parents wishing they'd paid more attention to what their children were doing before they ran away, joined a gang, robbed stores, or even murdered someone.

"So, just to be clear. You don't believe your daughter left because she was going to be let go?"

The woman's shoulders sagged. "I don't think she left. I think something bad happened to her. I just hope it isn't something horrible like what happened to the senator's wife."

Yes, Charlie did, too.

It was all Charlie could think about after they finished, and as she drove to the address the woman had given her for Bunny in Livonia on the Westside. Mrs. Powers hadn't written an apartment number, but Charlie found the name BUNNY ARCHER listed on the mailbox. Number 315. Another name had been crossed off and was unreadable. Mia's name, maybe?

Inside, two scrawny cats darted past her and another stretched out in the sun on the stairwell landing. The hallway smelled of cigarette smoke and cat urine. No one answered when she rang the apartment, but just as Charlie was about to leave, she saw a petite, elderly lady in sweatpants, sweatshirt and slippers standing in a doorway down the hall. Watching.

Oh, please...be a nosey neighbor. Charlie walked over. "Excuse me. Do you know the manager here?"

The woman crossed her arms. "I do. I'm the manager."

"Oh, good. I was supposed to meet my friend Bunny. And now she's not answering her phone or the door. Did you happen to see her leave or talk to her? I need to know when she might come back."

The woman's eyes narrowed. "Why would she tell you to meet her when she goes to work at this time?"

It was late afternoon. Whatever job Bunny had, it started late in the day. "Oh, she probably had a day off. We haven't talked for a long time and only exchanged a couple emails. We were going to catch up today."

"She's a hard one to keep track of. That girl is always changin' jobs," the manager said.

Interesting. "Since you're the manager, you must have known her former roommate then. Mia Powers. She's a friend of mine, too. I was trying to get in touch about a class reunion."

"The only roommate, besides the men, left a long time ago. And if you mean the blonde, no I didn't. She kep' to herself. They worked together at some exotic dance club. That's all I know."

The *blonde.* Had to be Mia.

"Thank you, so much," Charlie said. "It helps a lot." She frowned. "You know, now that I think about it, she might have told me to meet her where she works, but I can't remember the name of it. Do you happen to know?"

"Lady, half the time I don't even know my own

name. But I know a good looking man when I see one. And those girls had plenty comin' around."

Interesting times two. All Charlie had wanted to do was find Mia and get the information to get the senator off the hook, but the story kept changing and she'd done enough investigating to recognize there was more going on than met the eye. "Did you happen to see a tall, middle-aged man? Graying at the temples." She touched her own temples.

"Sure. Lots of them."

Shit.

"The one I saw the most was that senator with the bird's name."

"Senator Hawker?"

"Tall, gray at the temples. He be the one. Saw him a few weeks ago."

Visiting Bunny? Odd. Was he still trying to locate Mia, maybe?

"I haven't seen anyone in the past couple of weeks, though. Not even Bunny. She better be around when the rent's due, or she'll get the boot."

The easiest thing to do would be to call the senator and ask what was going on. If he'd met Mia in a club, and he'd hired an investigator to find her, as he'd said, the investigator would've gone to the club and talked to her co-workers. A good investigator would've talked to the apartment manager.

The manager turned and reached to close the door.

"Ma'am?"

The woman stopped. Looked at Charlie.

"One more question, if you don't mind. Has anyone else been here asking questions about Bunny and her former roommate?"

"You mean like the po-lice?"

Charlie's instincts said the woman was a smart lady, possibly getting her kicks from stringing along the stupid white girl. "No…just anyone."

"Nope. That much I know for sure. No one's been here askin' questions but you. And I know you ain't no friend of hers, so I'm not sayin' no more."

Charlie smiled and thanked the manager for her time. On the way downstairs, she punched in Max's number.

"Do me a favor," she said when she got Max on the line. "Take a look at the information I gave you and see if the senator lists Mia Power's former place of employment."

He was silent for a moment, papers shuffling. Max worked from a rented office in a building in center city Detroit that had been auctioned off and parts of it remodeled for rental. The building was inhabited mostly by artists. Max rented one small room, and she suspected his business wasn't all that good. Not the paying customers, anyway.

"Nothing here."

"Okay. Do you have any idea what exotic dance club a senator might frequent?" She had two choices. Wait for Bunny to come home, which could be a long time since the manager hadn't seen her for a while, or go to every strip club in Detroit to find her. Both options sucked.

Less than five seconds later, Max said, "Trumpps, on Eight Mile."

"Any others?" She had a few hours before the bars closed. She could hit at least three if they weren't too far apart.

"Top four… Trumpps, The Pantheon Club, Crazy Horse, and the Centerfold."

"Not Larry Flynt's Hustler?"

"Not in my book. The ratings aren't as high."

"You're awfully knowledgeable about strip clubs."

"All just a part of the PI landscape."

She thanked him, hung up, and headed for Trumpps. Start at the top and work her way down.

CHAPTER FIVE

THE GENTLEMEN'S CLUB, as Max had called it, teemed with lust-worthy women and horny men. She had to admit, the women she'd seen, so far, were elegant and sexy, unlike those in the strip joints she'd been to with her girlfriends in college. She remembered one sleazy club in particular because the dancer had to stop in the middle of the act and change her own music.

Glad she was wearing her work clothes, but wishing she'd worn pants with the jacket instead of the short skirt, Charlie bumped her way through the crowd and went directly to the bar. She wasn't about to sit there all night and wait for Bunny to show up on stage.

Not even a minute later, she sensed a presence behind her.

"Can I buy you a drink, *bonita?*"

She swung around. *Luc!* What the hell... was he still following her? Persistent jerk. And he needed to stop calling her *bonita*. Especially in a tone of voice that made it sound so seductive. "Still following me, I see."

"I could say I'm just making sure you don't get into any trouble. But—" he pulled the napkin out of his pocket "—what I really want is to follow up on your message."

So smug. So sure of himself. She laughed. "Not in *my* lifetime."

He placed a hand over his heart. "You wound me, *querida*." His soft brown gaze went from sexy to sorrowful puppy dog. "But I will stay here anyway to protect you. People who frequent this type of establishment might like the stage scenery, but in reality they're looking for someone like you to take home."

"Like me?" She couldn't help but want to hear where he'd go from there.

"Of course. The women on the stage tease and show off what they have to make a man lust after them. But they are the lazy men. Boys. Once, and he's done. A beautiful woman who hides her assets also hides the fire inside. She attracts the real man. One who wants to take his time making love to her...and touch her in all the right places. He wants to please her and not the other way around."

Her breathing deepened.

"It is a lot more effort and requires skill, but a man knows when it happens with the right woman, it is worth much more than time or money."

Was he joking? He actually seemed serious. "I—" Someone jostled her from behind, a hand landed on her butt...and squeezed. She squealed and jumped like a startled cat...right into the bodyguard's arms. He pulled her closer.

"Ah, so quick. I am surprised." He smiled. "But delighted."

Charlie jerked away, rounded on the butt grabber and elbowed him in the stomach. "Keep your hands to yourself, dude, or my boyfriend here will beat the shit out of you."

The guy glanced at Luc and raised his hands. "Sorry, man. I didn't know..."

She glanced at Luc, saw his eyebrows raise a hair.

"You see. I was right," Luc said, his mouth tipping up at the edges.

"Right about what?"

"About the fire inside. Yes?"

Fuck yes. And if she didn't put it out, she'd end up with the bodyguard doing her on the bar. "No, not yes. Not even if your boss wasn't my client. So, if you'll please leave me alone, I have a job to do."

"I can help if you'd like."

"And what is it that you think I need help with?"

"It doesn't matter. For starters, I'm a great bodyguard." Luc looked around. "And I believe you might need me tonight."

Charlie did. But not as a bodyguard. Not in the traditional sense anyway. Her hormones were screaming to be sated, and if it didn't happen soon, she couldn't be held responsible for whoever ended up in her bed.

But she had work to do, and he worked for the senator. It wouldn't hurt to have a strong man at her side for a few minutes. Even just to keep the butt grabbers away.

She turned toward the bar. The bartender was still there, apparently getting an earful.

"What can I get for you, ma'am?"

Ma'am? Geezus, she was barely thirty. She cleared her throat. "A Cosmo for me."

Luc grinned, turned to the bartender. "Burdeos."

The bartender shook his head as if he had no clue. She did. One of her former RB&B clients drank it for breakfast. Gran Patron Burdeos was one of the most expensive tequilas on the market. At one hundred dollars a shot, Luc had expensive tastes. "The senator must pay very well," she said.

"A generous expense account." Luc glanced at the bottles behind the bar, again. "Añejo, then."

"Is it getting warm in here?" Charlie shook off her jacket. Her white tank fit her quite nicely and with the short black skirt, she could still turn a few heads. Right now it was the bartender's head she needed. She angled her chin upward, eyelids at half-mast as she looked him over.

"He's a boy," Luc said softly, leaning in next to her. "He wouldn't know what to do with a woman like you."

The subtext was clear. *Luc would.* And she believed him. But she wanted information from 'the boy' and it was obvious only one thing interested him. She removed the band from her ponytail and let her hair fall around her shoulders.

When the bartender finished pouring and turned around, his eyes zapped straight to her chest. "I have a question for you," she said, locking eyes and leaning forward on the bar. "I'm looking for a friend. Bunny Archer. Is she working tonight?"

He smiled, his gaze still attached to her boobs. You'd think seeing multiple pairs bouncing around every night, he'd get tired of looking. She motioned him upward, two fingers to her eyes. "Up here, baby."

He looked up, but instead of being embarrassed or apologetic, he jutted his chin. "I guess you're not a very close friend, or you'd know she quit a couple weeks ago."

"I've been away." She resumed her come-on voice. "I only recently moved back to Detroit. You don't happen to know where she's working now, do you?"

When he crossed his arms and didn't answer, Luc pulled out a twenty and laid it on the bar, keeping it under his fingers.

The boy's eyes lit. "Uh, yeah. I might." He tipped his head to the posters of several strippers along one wall. "Bunny's the third one on the left."

She looked at Luc who handed the kid his money.

Yeah, she just might have to take the bodyguard up on his offer to help her.

Luc was ready to leave the club when, after getting as much information as possible about Bunny, Charlie asked the bartender, "What do you know about Mia Powers?"

The bartender pulled Luc's twenty from his fingers sending the message that any more information was going to cost them more, too. Oh, how he'd love to teach the boy a lesson about greed, but it would have to be some other time.

Right now he wanted to keep the beautiful woman at his side happy. He pulled out another twenty. Shoved it forward. "Greed is a fat demon with a small mouth, and whatever you feed it is never enough."

The bartender's glazed look was typical. Few were as well versed as Luc, having been trained for years to be the best in his trade. That meant having a grand store of knowledge to draw upon for use when necessary. Tonight, it was necessary to impress the lovely Charlize, a much prettier name than her masculine nickname.

"Janwillem van de Wetering," he explained, knowing full well the Dutch author's name wasn't one the boy bartender would recognize. But he knew the senator's attorney had an interest in the former Zen student's writings. He knew most everything about Charlize Street.

Except what was in her head. The things he wanted most to know. Not only for the senator, but for himself.

Because for the first time since he could remember, he wondered what his life might have been like had he not been born Juan Carlos Guerrero, a bastard who'd grown up in *El Dompe* in Tijuana.

Had he not been trained to be a cold-blooded assassin.

The beautiful Charlize angled her head, letting him know she was impressed, however momentarily. She returned her gaze to the bartender. "Mia was Bunny's roommate a while ago. I understand Mia worked here, too."

Reaching for the money, a frown creased the bartender's brow. "You guys cops or something?"

"Answer the question, *pendejo.*" Luc slapped his hand over the bartender's and squeezed.

"Oww."

"I will let go when you answer the lady's question." Luc had the strength of Kratos and a vice grip so strong he could break the twit's hand with one quick squeeze. Trained in the deadliest martial arts of Silhat and Krav Maga, he was quick, athletic and could strike faster than the eye could blink. And sometimes it was good to remind people he was a dangerous man.

The boy's eyes bulged. "Mia Powers worked here a while back. She was involved with some older guy who had money. He bought her all kinds of shit, dressed her up like some society broad, until she thought she was too good to work here anymore and quit. Last I heard Bunny was working at the Centerfold. She still comes in once in a while to talk to the other girls." He took a breath. "That's all I know."

Luc squeezed one more time.

"Oh, man," the kid whined. "Yeah, yeah. I remember one of the girls saying Mia left a bunch of shit in her locker."

"Did anyone remove the contents of the locker?" Charlie asked.

"I don't know. You'd have to ask the manager." Tears formed in his eyes.

Once Luc let go, the bartender shook out his hand. Made a face. "Damn. That fucking hurt!"

Charlie launched to her feet. "Where's the manager's office?"

The bartender pointed to some stairs going to a mezzanine of sorts. "First door. He won't give it to you, though. Not unless you're family."

CHAPTER SIX

UPSTAIRS, CHARLIE SAW a light coming from underneath the first door. She heard voices and knocked.

"Go away. I'm busy," a man's voice shouted back.

"I'm here about Mia Powers…the things she left in her locker."

"Dammit." The same nasal voice. "Just a minute."

Luc had waited downstairs at the bar, and Charlie was glad. She didn't need him strong-arming anyone else. She hadn't gotten to the point of bribery yet, either, but Luc was obviously not as patient as she was.

A moment later, the door opened and a disheveled man without a shirt and his belt hanging unbuckled stood in the doorway. An equally disheveled and half-dressed woman lounged on a couch in the background, legs spread, arms crossed, and looking not too happy at being interrupted.

The man gave Charlie a once over. "I'm guessing you're not Mia's mother."

"Correct. My name is Charlie Street. I'm an attorney working on a case involving Mia Powers. I understand she left some things here in her locker."

"Bunny said Mia's mother was going to come and pick it up. I can't give it to a stranger." He kept one hand on the door and pulled it partway closed so she could no longer see the woman on the couch.

Esther Powers, Mia's mother hadn't said anything about picking up her daughter's things. In fact Esther didn't appear to even know her daughter had worked at the club. "Mrs. Powers can't make it and she's authorized me to pick it up and bring it to her."

He looked at her askance.

"Arty, get rid of whoever it is and get your ass back here."

Arty ran a hand through his hair. "Uh, yeah." He pulled out a cell phone. "Darla, there's a lady, an attorney, who's here to get the things in Mia Powers' locker. Miss …" he looked to Charlie.

"Street. Charlie Street."

Miss Street will be outside my office. Get over here and help her." He clicked off.

Nice guy.

"Darla will be right here." The door clicked shut in Charlie's face.

She laughed. Fine with her as long as she got what she wanted.

Within minutes a heavy-set woman of indeterminate age barreled down the hallway carrying a large purple and yellow duffle bag. Reaching Charlie, she held it out.

"Probably just her outfits, wigs and stuff like that. Guess she doesn't need it anymore or she'd have come and got it."

"Right. She has another type of job." Charlie thanked her, feeling no obligation to tell anyone anything. She took the bag and returned to the bar.

Luc was holding her jacket up, old school-like, to help her put it on. Something men used to do. She set the duffle bag on the stool, put one arm into a sleeve, then the other. Luc stood so close she could feel his warm breath against her cheek. When finished, he laid his hands on her shoulders, smoothed the fabric, each stroke like a caress. Then he gently lifted her hair from under the collar, his fingers grazing her neck. Goosebumps skittered over her skin.

She pulled away, grabbed the bag, and headed for the door.

"Thanks," she said over her shoulder on the way out. "And stop following me."

Luc pulled his silver Lexus CT200h, compliments of the senator, directly behind Charlie at The Centerfold Club on John R Street, a little south of Eight Mile. He'd intended to follow her home to make sure she got there safely. But apparently she wasn't satisfied with the information she'd gotten so far and wanted to talk to Bunny Archer, too.

"Really?" Charlie said as they both exited their cars in the parking lot. "What is it with you?"

"I am smitten, *bonita*. I cannot help myself."

"Unbelievable. What part of no do you not understand?"

"Just doing my job."

"Your job is to follow me around?"

"To be available for your needs on the senator's case. And I see a need to keep you safe. The streets of Detroit are not safe for a woman alone at night."

She raised her hands. "How have I managed all these years?"

As Luc opened the door of the establishment for Charlie, a sweet smell drifted outside and the heavy beat of 80s rock music blasted through the air. She rushed in, immediately went to the bar and instead of ordering a drink, she asked to talk to Bunny Archer. She oozed authority and confidence. A strong woman. Adaptable. He liked.

The bartender, an older man with the bloated, coarse complexion of a long-time drinker, said, "Who wants to know?"

"I need to talk to her. It's important."

His eyes narrowed. "You a cop?"

Charlie shook her head. "I'm Bunny's sister."

Again, impressive. Ms. Charlize lied convincingly. No hesitation whatsoever. She did not play by the rules, either. She would make a good assassin.

The bartender motioned one of the waitresses over. "Tell Margo that Bunny's *sister* is here." He looked at Luc and Charlie again. "What're you drinking?"

"Nothing for me," Charlie said.

Luc waved him off and turned to Charlie. "What if she doesn't have a sister?"

"If she does, she'll come out to see me, and if she doesn't, she'll come out to see who's posing as her sister. Win-win." She gave a satisfied smile.

Just then a petite black woman with bleached blond hair and gigantic enhanced breasts sashayed toward them. "Bunny Archer?" Charlie asked when the woman reached them.

"No. But I'm a friend. And I know she doesn't have a sister."

"You're right. But it's important that I get in contact with Bunny.

Luc watched the exchange and pulled some more bills from his pocket. The woman's eyes lit. He almost laughed. The underbelly of greed in the US was just as prevalent as it was in Mexico. A country where the rich got richer and the poor became poorer. The two countries were not so different. They just did the same things differently.

Taking the proffered twenty, the woman said, "Bunny came into some money about a week ago and split. Said she was going to live the good life from now on. Didn't tell anyone where she was going, but she left in a hurry. Like she didn't want anyone to know."

Music thumped in the background, heavy metal Led Zeppelin type songs that grated on Luc's sensibilities. His mother had loved classical and opera music and had played it all the time on the small record player she'd salvaged from the dump.

"Now I will follow you to make sure you get home okay," Luc said when Charlie was finally ready to go and they went to their cars outside. "And you can show me what is in the bag."

CHAPTER SEVEN

"IT'S A HYPOTHETICAL QUESTION, Alan. That's all."

"Okay. But since I know you're representing Senator Hawker, it's difficult for me to not go there." He raised a brow. "It's also difficult for me not to notice how great you look. Working for the big boys seems to agree with you, and I have to say that surprises me."

"Probably no more of a surprise than me seeing you working here."

"Touché." He sighed. "So much for college student idealism." He motioned to the chair in front of his desk and then sat in the seat next to her.

"Speak for yourself. My slide into the dark side is only temporary."

Alan cocked his head in question. Still as handsome as when they were lovers in college. When they both dreamed of saving the world.

"I haven't given up my plans," she said. "They just got detoured for a bit."

He reached over and placed a hand on hers. "You still trying to piece together what happened to your father and bring the bad guys to justice. I heard that was the reason you were asked to leave your job with the department. Heard you were getting into some deep waters with the P.D., too."

Her nerves twitched. "That's not why I'm here."

"Right. You're here to ask me hypothetical questions that I'm supposed to think are not about Senator Hawker's case." He smiled.

She pulled away. Couldn't help smiling back. "Right." He knew her so well. They'd been so perfect together. Sometimes she still had a hard time imagining what had gone wrong. But it had. Horribly so. And it had taken a long time to truly get over it. Get over him.

"Okay, what's the hypothetical?"

She'd gone over it in her mind a dozen times figuring out the best way to get an answer without giving away the store. "Okay, let's say I somehow got some information about a client that said client hadn't disclosed, and which made me think the client wasn't telling me the truth about some things, and said information might implicate him in a crime that has nothing to do with the case I've taken. Would I need to disclose that to him?"

Alan frowned. Steepled his hands. "I would think you'd want to so you could work with a clean slate."

Yeah. No surprises. Surprises were an attorney's worst nightmare. If a client withheld information or didn't tell the truth about even one thing, how could you believe them on anything else? She ran a hand through her hair.

"But you didn't need me to tell you that. What else?"

"And if I learned something that was potentially against the law, it would have to remain confidential. Attorney client privilege." Now she was simply talking to herself.

Standing, Alan looked at his watch. "You really didn't need me for this, did you."

It wasn't a question. Charlie stood, too. Sighed. He was right. She just wanted to hear someone knowledgeable say something different. Give her a way out. She laughed. "No, I guess not. But since I'm here, I can personally congratulate you on the assistant A.G. position. One more step and you'll be where you want to be."

He grinned and took both of her hands in his. "Have dinner with me later and help me celebrate."

Charlie's stomach rolled. There was a time when she would've liked nothing more.

"Things are so different now," he said. "We used to be so good together."

They had been good together. Most of the time.

"And now we're both good with someone else," Charlie said.

He shook his head. "Marcy and I are getting a divorce." He looked at her hand. "You're not married, are you?"

"Not yet." And she doubted she ever would be.

"Not yet sounds like someone's not stepping up to the plate."

"Not yet because there's no batter and I hate baseball. It's a slow game that gets your hopes up and then crushes them at the end."

He frowned, pulled back. "Oh-kay. Message received."

Laughing, she reached out and touched his arm. "Nothing personal in that, Alan. Really. Work is my priority right now and I need to keep it that way." She had to focus. Not get caught up in old friendships that had the potential to turn into something more. Something that would use up all her oxygen. Stifle her desire to be more, do more. Make a difference.

CHAPTER EIGHT

"JEAN-LUC FONTAINEBLEAU," MAX SAID. "He was good friends with both Mia Powers and Bunny Archer."

"Okay, it's another lead, but did you get anything on Bunny? If anyone has a clue where Mia went it would be her roommate. My research indicates they were friends for years." Charlie drummed her fingers on her desk at RB&B.

Her office was all dark wood and wall-to-wall glass. On the thirty-fifth floor in the RenCen Tower, she had a grand view of the Detroit River and the city of Windsor, Canada, on the other side. A far cry from her dream and not in a good way.

She couldn't wait to buy the small abandoned hotel not too far from the old Michigan Central train station. The dilapidated hotel property was owned by the city and would be up for auction within the year. All she had to do was amass enough money to bid on it and then remodel.

"The women may have been friends for years, but it doesn't necessarily mean they had any contact outside of work and living together," Max said, bringing her to the moment.

"True. But since we don't know, we need to find Bunny Archer and find out. I'm also wondering who left Bunny enough money to quit working and live like a queen."

"One of her wealthy clients at the strip club where she worked, maybe?"

"Possible." Or someone who wanted her out of the picture so she wouldn't talk to anyone about her old roommate. She remembered what Bunny's apartment manager had said about Senator Hawker visiting Bunny a few weeks ago. Whenever Charlie thought of one possibility, another popped up. The senator's case was becoming far more complex than had been indicated.

And something was off. People didn't disappear and steal records without a reason and a few came to mind. One, Mia Powers was embezzling money and skipped to protect herself when the senator decided he wanted a younger model. Or, two, as Mia's mother feared, something bad had happened to Mia. Or three, Mia had sold or given the records to the senator's opponent to make him look bad.

If Mia's disappearance was from an accident or a random abduction, it wouldn't account for the missing records. Which gave rise to another theory. Mia knew too much and someone needed to get rid of both Mia and the records. Not a scenario she wanted to entertain.

"I'm meeting with Esther Powers today to give her the bag with Mia's things in it. There could be some clue to where she went."

"You didn't peek inside?"

"Nope." She grinned remembering the look on Luc's face when he'd followed her out of the Centerfold strip club and she'd told him she wasn't going to open the bag. Said it wasn't ethical. Never mind that she'd lied to get it. Those were two different situations. One necessary, the other was not. "I'll find out soon enough." She glanced at the clock. "In fact, I better get moving."

Charlie hung up, thankful she had Max to bounce ideas off. They connected on so many levels, she had to admit she'd envisioned more than a business or friend relationship on an occasion or two. She grinned, that was never going to happen. She knew better than to ruin a good thing. She gathered her things, ready to close up shop and head to Esther Powers' home when Douglas Reston appeared in the doorway.

"Got a minute?"

"Of course. Come in." Charlie motioned for him to sit. He came over, placed his hands on the back of the chair and stood there towering over her. The power stance.

Douglas was a nice man. They'd worked together in the past. She'd saved his butt a couple of times when he was going the wrong direction on a case, so he'd given her a chance when no other firm was interested after her so-called resignation from the Public Defender's Office.

She owed Douglas, but he was totally blind when it came to ethics. As long as the cash kept coming in, he didn't give a rat's ass whether it was clean money or not.

"You know Senator Hawker is not only a client, but he and I are also old friends."

"Yes, I do." He'd told her dozens of times, including long before he'd hired her.

"And it's important we do the best job we can to keep our clients happy."

"Of course. And I've been doing everything I can to get the necessary information to keep the senator from being indicted. In fact, last night I came upon some information that could lead me to the woman who has his records."

"What information?"

She told him about Mia Powers' secret past, and

Bunny Archer, and the upcoming meeting with Esther Powers later in the afternoon. She didn't mention the duffle bag. He'd want to see it, maybe even give it to the senator.

He rubbed his knuckles against his chin.

"I'm hoping this information could be exactly what we need to close this thing up."

Douglas gave her a worried smile.

What wasn't he telling her? "Is there something else I need to know?"

"No, no," he said. "But if you find out anything important, bring it to me before doing anything. Senator Hawker's getting unnerved by this whole thing, so we need to keep him apprised of what's going on."

"Sure." She glanced at the time again. "I better go. I don't want to miss my appointment with Mrs. Powers."

Thirty minutes later, Charlie pulled into Esther Powers' drive and wondered again why Mia had been working in a strip club when the family had so much money. Surely they would've helped their daughter if she needed it.

Mrs. Powers, dressed in a white silk shirt, black slacks and black suede flats, greeted Charlie at the door, and instead of going to the small parlor as before, she invited Charlie into the family room where she had a toasty fire going in the fireplace. The open concept layout included the kitchen, which looked as if it had been recently renovated exactly like one you'd find on an HGTV program.

A humungous granite topped island with a built-in wine rack and cooler underneath was the focal point of the room. Another humungous granite topped breakfast bar with six stools took up one whole side of the room. A wall of windows spread across the entire width of the house making the swimming pool, gazebo and Tuscan garden patio visible.

And Mrs. Powers seemed to be the only one there.

The sharp contrast between the opulence in some areas of the city and the total devastation in others just minutes away gave new meaning to the old cliché…so near, and yet so far.

"I'm having a glass of wine. Would you like one?" She indicated the coffee table with a bottle of wine and a crystal wine glass setting on top.

"No thank you." She'd love one, but it would have to be later when she wasn't driving anywhere. Charlie removed the duffle strap from her shoulder and handed the bag to Mrs. Powers. "This was in Mia's locker at her former place of employment. I didn't open it, but I would like to see if there's anything in it that will give me a clue to what might've happened."

"Of course." Mrs. Powers motioned Charlie to sit, then set the bag on the coffee table next to a package of *Esse Black* cigarettes, sat, too, and then quickly poured herself a glass of red wine. "I'm sorry. Ever since you called, I've been preparing myself for the worst. Maybe there's a suicide note in it, or something awful I don't want to know about."

Well, there was that. "Is your husband—"

"No. He's out of town working. He's always out of town."

"Was your daughter depressed?"

"I don't know. I told you she didn't stay in touch once she started with that man." She looked at the bag like it might be contaminated with the Ebola virus and she didn't want to get too close.

Would you like me to open it?"

"I would appreciate it very much."

Charlie scooted to the edge of the couch cushion so she could reach the coffee table. The bag was heavy, so she figured there must be shoes and other things in it besides the skimpy costumes the dancers wore. If Mrs.

Powers didn't know her daughter was a stripper, this could indeed be a shock. "Let's keep our fingers crossed that whatever is inside, it's something to help us find Mia."

And on that note, Charlie unzipped the bag. Inside were some wigs, sequined dancer's clothes, tassels, fur-lined handcuffs and other exotic paraphernalia, a couple pairs of glitter-speckled mile-high platform stilettos, some makeup, hair dryer, a few old photos and a plastic bag of costume jewelry. At the bottom was a black velvet box and inside, a sparkly necklace.

Charlie took it out of the box and held it up. A very expensive diamond necklace.

It made sense that Mia wouldn't want to wear the necklace while dancing, but she could think of only one reason someone would leave an expensive item like a diamond necklace in a locker at a strip club. And it wasn't good. "Have you seen this before?"

Eyes wide, Mrs. Powers shook her head.

The woman was clearly surprised, and no doubt shocked. The whole thing had to be a shock. Charlie had hoped Mrs. Powers had given her daughter the necklace. That would answer that question. But if Mia's mother hadn't given her the necklace, where did she get it?

Charlie picked up the photos, most of which had been taken with the girls at the club, handed them to Mrs. Powers one by one after looking herself.

"Oh, it's Addy. Adeline Archer," Mrs. Powers said, apparently not as shocked by the things in her daughter's stash as Charlie thought. Charlie glanced at the photo. Two teenage girls, sweet and innocent. Adeline, she realized was also known as Bunny. But apparently, Esther Powers didn't know.

From the early photos, it looked like Bunny had natural platinum blond hair and Mia had dark hair, unlike her blond mother. From the photos she'd seen of Mia, she'd become a blonde after college. Mia probably had a stage name, too.

"What about this one?" Charlie held up a photo of a youngish, maybe college-aged Mia standing with a young man near a fireplace at a cabin.

"Oh, that's Jean-Luc. He and Mia were best friends all through college. She knew he was...different. And the poor boy was so tortured over it, he had a breakdown in his third year and left school. Mia lost track of him afterward, but then one night he called here. Apparently Mia had left him a message and he was returning the call. He didn't know she wasn't living here anymore."

"When was the call?"

"Last year. Not too long before Mia disappeared."

"The senator believes she deliberately ran away."

"I hate that man. He only cares about himself."

Esther Powers dislike for the senator went deep. "Did you know the senator?"

"No, not personally. He wouldn't even talk to me when I wanted him to help me look for Mia. He said she deserved whatever happened to her."

Charlie could see the senator being upset about his records being stolen, but to be that unsympathetic toward a woman who didn't know where her daughter was seemed out of character. Having the same experience with his son, he had to know how Mrs. Powers must be feeling...and be more sympathetic.

"Is that it?" Mrs. Powers asked.

It seemed that way. She didn't see anything else in the bag, so Charlie turned it upside down just to be sure. Something rattled. She glanced inside. Nothing. The bag was still heavier than any duffle Charlie owned, and she shook it again. Another rattle. A secret compartment?

Feeling around the bottom, she felt something hard and square between the canvas and the cardboard bottom.

"I don't want it."

"Excuse me?"

"I don't want those…those clothes….all that stuff I knew nothing about. It's as if my daughter led two different lives…and I didn't even know her. My own daughter and I didn't know her." Her tone alternated between hurt, accusing and incredulous. She gulped the rest of her wine. "Take it away. Get rid of it." She waved a hand as if she could whisk away the unpleasantness.

There was something else in the bag, something that had gotten stuck between the bottom and the outer canvas…or something deliberately hidden, Charlie was sure of it.

"What would you like me to do with it?" Charlie stuffed everything back in the bag, except the photos and diamond necklace. "The necklace is worth a lot of money." *A bundle*.

"Never mind. I'll get rid of this trash myself." She rose, wavered a little, the wine apparently doing its job, then caught herself with a hand on the chair. She snatched up the duffle before Charlie had a chance to protest, then stumbled across the room to the fireplace. "This is exactly where all this horrible stuff belongs."

CHAPTER NINE

"NO!" CHARLIE SHOT to her feet, ran over and grabbed the bag from Mrs. Powers just as it left the woman's fingertips. "You can't destroy evidence."

Esther reached to take the bag from Charlie.

Charlie crushed it against her chest and crossed her arms. "You filed a missing person's report, didn't you?"

The woman nodded.

"Well, this bag could be evidence for the police. If they haven't been looking for your daughter all this time because they think she just wanted to go away somewhere. This bag indicates something different."

"It's just slutty clothes." Her words slurred.

How much wine had this woman had before Charlie arrived? "The clothes and the other contents indicate something isn't right. I mean…who would leave a very expensive necklace in a gym bag and not return to get it?" When she got no response, Charlie added, "I think someone needs to check it out."

"Hah!" The woman raised her hands nearly sloshing wine on her silk shirt. "The police won't do anything."

Charlie wasn't a Detroit PD fan, either. With over three hundred murders a year, and a city crumbling in on itself, Detroit was bankrupt in more ways than one.

And while there were honest cops out there, the police were overworked, underpaid and underfunded. She'd worked in the court system long enough to know some were on the take and others were in bed with the mafia and drug cartels.

And they'd lied to her when they'd arrested her father. They'd treated him like scum and were as responsible for his murder as much as if they'd pulled the trigger.

Her stomach knotted every time she thought about it. "You don't know that the police won't do anything."

"Then you take it to them. Do whatever you want with it." Mrs. Powers flapped a hand in dismissal before raising a wrist to her forehead like a southern belle about to swoon. She stumbled to the couch and plunked her ass in the squishy cushions.

"You're sure?" Charlie held up the bag.

"Please. I need to rest now."

Mrs. P had a problem. Addicts were easy to recognize. Probably pills and alcohol.

She didn't know how Mrs. P would feel about her decision in the morning, but not wanting to leave the evidence in the hands of chance, Charlie stuffed the photos and necklace in her purse, thanked Mrs. Powers for talking with her, grabbed the duffle and hightailed it out of there.

She'd take it to the police as requested.

After she found out what was in the bottom of the bag.

Driving away, Charlie saw the lights in the Powers' house go off and felt a kernel of guilt for leaving the woman alone. She'd probably fall asleep with a bottle and a cigarette in her hands or OD on some pills. Although she hadn't smelled cigarettes in the house, so the woman probably smoked outside. That was good.

If one could call anything about Mrs. Ps life good.

Her husband was out of town, her daughter was missing, and she was all alone in a house big enough to be a museum. If Charlie ever became envious of those who had more, all she needed to do was remember Mrs. Powers.

A good forty minutes from home, her curiosity getting the better of her, Charlie drove to the nearest Seven Eleven, pulled into the lighted parking area and parked on the end, away from the other cars.

Leaving her car running, she rummaged in the glove compartment and found her handy-dandy tool that had multiple instruments on it, including a mini-foldout scissors, a screwdriver, and a tiny knife. Deciding on the knife, she flipped over the bag, made a slit on one end, and slid her hand inside. Hit something hard.

Hah. She was right. Something hard and square, about the size of a CD, and maybe a half-inch thick. Pulling it out she frowned. Whatever it was had been wrapped in tan postal paper and heavy packaging tape. She stuck her hand inside the opening, again. Nothing else.

Studying the package, she turned it over. No address, no nothing. And she couldn't open it without ruining the wrapping. Whatever was in the package had to be important, otherwise why would Mia Powers go to all the trouble?

If she took everything to the police as is, without opening the package, she may never know what was inside.

More customers pulled in, and a few seconds later a green sedan drove in and parked next to her. Two men. The one in the passenger seat looked directly at her. Her heartbeat quickened as if she was doing something illegal.

She shoved the package inside her purse where she'd put the other non-slutty items, then tossed the duffle on the passenger seat. The police wouldn't do anything with the information tonight, so she might as well go home. Douglas had asked her to keep him informed, too, so she would do it when she got there. Or wait until she went to the office in the morning.

Just as she looked down and reached to put the car in gear, a loud *bang* rattled the driver's window. She jumped, let out a small shriek, and turning, saw the man from the car next to her directly outside her window motioning for her to open the door.

Her pulse skyrocketed. *No way in hell, buddy.* She shook her head. Reached for the shift, and heard another *bang* on the passenger side. She jumped again.

Oh, shit. Another guy. He grabbed the door handle and yanked. *Shit, shit, shit.*

Glad she always kept her doors locked, she fumbled to put the car in gear… saw in her peripheral vision the man on her right raise a long black rod.

The stupid shift wouldn't move. Damn! She jiggled it, again.

The window resisted his first blow but shattered into tiny pieces on the second. Finally in gear, she floored the accelerator just as the man snatched the duffle from the front seat. Her car screeched in reverse, nearly tearing his arm off as he yanked the bag away.

Tires squealing, she changed gears, burned rubber out the driveway, and sped down Moross Road toward I-94. *Oh, God. Oh, God. Breathe, breathe*, she repeated until she was on the freeway. Her best guess said those goons weren't looking for some wigs, thongs, nipple tassels and sparkly stilettos…and it wasn't going to take long for them to realize that's all they had.

If she stayed on the freeway, they would eventually catch up. She sped past a couple of exits, the chill wind blowing in through the broken window, stinging her face.

Any exit coming up soon was going to take her into some questionable areas, but she had to get off the freeway, find an out-of-the-way place to regroup and decide what to do. One thing was sure, if she stayed on the freeway, she was an open target.

Another sign flashed by. The Outer Drive exit was next. Charlie merged over two lanes, cutting off more than one car. Horns blared and honked, crazed sounds following her as she sped onto the exit. All she needed was a little time to get her phone and call the police.

The first street sign she saw was Harper Avenue. She continued west on Harper until she saw a Harper Food Store sign. A public place. Yeah. She whipped into the food store parking lot and found a space on the right side of a van that conveniently hid her smaller vehicle.

Charlie's heart raced. She reached for her purse. Whatever Mia had hidden in the bag was important enough for someone to send a couple of thugs to steal it. She glanced up as a man walked by, hands in his pockets, hood over his head. Not him. But without a window, she was vulnerable to more than theft.

Pulling out her phone, Luc's business card slid out with it. Hah! This was one night when she would've been happy if he'd followed her. She'd feel a lot safer right now.

Those men had to have been watching Esther Powers' house, because otherwise how would anyone know Charlie even had the bag? Only one other person besides Mrs. Powers knew she had it. Luc. And she only knew of one person who had a vested interest in the contents of Mia's bag. Her client.

She could be wrong, but…

She turned on her phone, then texted, I'M COMING OVER.

CHAPTER TEN

"I DON'T KNOW who to trust, Landon. Douglas is my friend. I would be sleeping on the streets if he hadn't hired me."

"That's a bit overly dramatic, isn't it? I mean you could've stayed with me or with Mom."

Her little brother could be so obtuse at times. "Right. But Douglas did me a favor and I owe it to him to do the job he hired me to do."

"Which is?"

"Help the client prove his innocence."

"Even if he's not."

It wasn't a question. "He is." She hoped. "I have to believe he is, but that's not the problem. The problem is that when I'm trying to do my job, other stuff comes up and puts me in a sticky situation." Her brother knew she was representing the senator—anyone who watched the news knew it. But she couldn't tell her brother anything specific about the case because everything else was confidential. Attorney, client confidentiality.

Landon stretched out in his chair at the Seventh Street Boxing Gym. Once he'd turned eighteen, he'd taken over their father's business from their uncle, Emilio, who had run the no-frills gym since their father died, twenty-two years ago. Landon and Uncle Emilio still carried out the mentoring program her dad had started to help keep the neighborhood youth busy and off the streets. Charlie was more at home at the gym than she was in the condo she'd purchased a year ago…when she'd had what she thought was a secure job.

"Stuff comes up. Such as?" He teepeed his hands. "Theoretically."

"Theoretically, such as me finding incriminating information about the client that doesn't have anything to do with the crime he allegedly committed, but could be worse.

"Tell your boss. He'll take you off the case."

"That's the other problem. I don't want to be off the case." She didn't have a choice. Not if she wanted to continue eating. "And it is just theoretically. I don't really expect to find something incriminating." But she was a little less sure than she'd been in the beginning.

Landon frowned. Still sweaty after sparring with one of the guys at the gym, his hair looped in curls onto his forehead. With their father's dark hair and complexion and their mother's sky blue eyes, her brother was seriously handsome beyond compare.

"Okay. If confusing me is what you wanted to do, you've succeeded."

Charlie spread out, lounging on the cot in Landon's office, a no-nonsense room with concrete floor and walls and only his own graffiti art as decoration. "I know. I've confused myself. I just need time to figure some out some things. And right now, I don't seem to have time."

"What's stopping you?"

Two thugs who wanted something she had, so she didn't dare go home. "I have something someone wants. I don't know what it is, but it's part of the reason I don't want to tell anyone, and also why I don't want to let the case go."

Landon narrowed his gaze. "I must be just as whacked as you because I think I actually understood all of that. How bad do they want it?"

"Bad enough to break my car window to get it."

"And they didn't?" He leaned forward, arms crossed on the desk. "Get it, I mean."

"No, they thought they did, and by now they've figured out they didn't. And now I have the additional problem of driving a car in downtown Detroit without a window."

Her brother grimaced, a look she was familiar with. Landon was her sounding board, her go-to person whenever she needed to talk something over with someone.

"Damn, you do have a problem or two. So, okay...use one of my cars and stash the goods someplace. As soon as they know you don't have it—"

"They'll break my fingers to get it. Or worse."

"Do you know that?"

"No, but I don't not know it, either."

"Okay, toss a decoy in the river and tell them to go get it."

Her brother was a typical guy in wanting to tell her how to fix the problem when what she wanted was to talk it out so she could come up with her own answers. However, his idea was a pretty good one. One other little problem was, she didn't know what she had, so it was hard to judge the extent of the danger. The package could be something totally innocuous and whoever wanted it would be just as surprised to find it was nothing.

"Or you could get a bodyguard until you know what to do with the stuff."

Another pretty good idea. One she'd already thought of, but in a more self-serving way.

Luc was working for the senator and if he could help her, why not. "I could, but..." But she'd told Mrs.

Powers she would take it to the police, another situation that could cause more problems than not.

Not only had the Detroit PD had been battling bad cop syndrome and internal corruption for years, she'd been pestering them for years about her father's case. They were never happy to see her and the feeling was more than mutual. At one point, she'd all but been ordered by the chief of police to stay away.

But what if the package held something important in her efforts to find Mia? The senator's records were critical since they could make the allegations against him go away. She hoped.

Okay. Decision made. She'd look at what was in the package and *then* take it to the police. The necklace, too. Maybe. Depending on what was in the package.

She launched to her feet. "I know what to do."

Landon cracked a big white smile, making him look even more like their father, a man her brother barely remembered. Being three years younger than Charlie, Landon was only five when their father had been arrested. *Framed. Murdered.*

"So spit it out." Landon stood, too.

He was at least six-feet two inches, the tallest in their family and seemed to tower over her, even though, with heels, she was five-ten or taller.

"Or do I have to guess? No, wait…let me, because I know."

"You don't know. How would you know?"

"You're going to open the package and then decide."

Charlie looked at him askance. "Lucky guess."

They both laughed. "Okay," Landon said. "There's something else I need to talk to you about."

His expression pinched. "It's Mom."

Charlie's phone vibrated. She pulled it from her pocket and glanced at the caller ID.

No name, but the number looked familiar. She remembered the business card.

Luc. Lucas Cabrera.

She let it go to message, watched it click off. "Uh, yeah. Can that talk wait just a little? I really, really need to concentrate on this case. How about a drink one night this week. You can come over or we can go somewhere."

He eyed her narrowly. "Should I hire a bodyguard for you?"

"No, I know someone. A couple people in fact." She gave him a look. "Seriously. I'll be fine."

He sat back and after a moment, said, "Okay. So, where is it? Let's open it and see what you got. She pulled a chair to Landon's desk. He brought a chair next to her.

Charlie took the package out of her purse.

Looking at it, Landon said, "You know, it could just be a movie or CDs.

"Could be. But it looks like something Mia was going to mail to someone."

Landon grabbed the package, looked it over and took out a small scissors from his desk drawer. "I'm doing this."

"Go for it."

The package was double wrapped, but it took only a few minutes to peel away the stiff postal paper and a thin layer of bubble wrap. Landon held up a black plastic box that looked to be about four-by-six inches and maybe an inch deep. "It's a portable, external hard drive," he said, showing her one end. "See, here's the spot for a USB cord."

The senator's files? If so, the information could be exactly what she needed to clear up the allegations against her client. *Or go the other way.*

"So, let's see what's on it." Landon rubbed his hands together, got up and went to a metal filing cabinet in the corner and pulled out a cord. "Perfect."

"What?"

"I'll plug this puppy into my laptop and we'll know what's on it."

"Okay." Only she wasn't sure Landon should see what was on it. As far as she knew, it was Mia's property, not her client's, but she had come upon it while working on his case. "Let me look at it first."

He handed her the cord. "Be my guest."

Charlie drew the laptop toward her, plugged one end into the computer and the other into the hard drive. And waited. It took a few seconds and then a bar popped up on the monitor.

"Oh, crap. I need a password."

Charlie's phone rang again.

No answer. Of course not. She was a smart woman.

Too smart to be taken in by the senator's sweet-talking bodyguard. But she liked him, he was certain. All he had to do was convince her he was one of the good guys.

Having the senator's blessing to keep an eye on the *chica bonita* couldn't have worked more perfectly into his plans. He would keep the senator happy and also make sure the lovely Charlize wouldn't mess up his hunting plans.

Fresh from his shower, he was observing her apartment from his apartment across the street when he saw two men. Recognized them. They weren't the two at the Greektown Casino when Charlie was at the poker table. They were the two he'd spotted at Trumpps when Charlie had left his side to talk with the club manager. Now they were here watching her apartment building. Waiting for her to return.

Like he was.

What he hadn't nailed down was whether they were local LEOs, FBI, or Detroit mafia. The difference between the groups, other than who they worked for, wasn't much these days, but it made a difference in what they might want from her. Or want to do to her.

The goons had been easy to spot. Blackout had trained him well. The government agency he worked for, Black O.U.T., was so secret only two people within the government knew of its existence. And neither were the president. If Luc failed on a job and got caught, no one knew *he* existed.

The operatives didn't even know each other, although he'd crossed paths with more than a few. More highly trained than any other government forces, he and his compatriots were considered the most lethal human weapons the United States government possessed.

The *Bourne Identity* wasn't just fiction scripted for an action movie. Dark ops programs of some kind existed in most countries. Some were just better than others...and better at hiding them.

Although he had to be available on the spot if called for a job, he had both autonomy and anonymity. He had a huge store of funds and multiple identities and was able to travel at whim. A life many would envy.

Despite all that, he'd never quite been able to reconcile the life of a government assassin with his basic needs. It was a lonely life.

But whoever was paying the way for these two *imbeciles* weren't getting their money's worth. It had to be the senator they were spying on and not the lovely Charlize, but if either one of those goons attempted to harm her—the *pendejo* would not live to regret it.

He paced in front of his window, glanced at the time. Ten p.m. She was usually home long before now.

He picked up the phone and called again.

"Charlie Street," came the answer.

Luc's spirits soared. "Hello, *bonita*. I am happy to hear your sweet voice."

"Chill, Romeo. I need to talk with you. Can you meet me right now?"

"Anytime, anywhere, anyplace, *querida*."

She gave him an address, which from his research a few weeks ago, he recognized as her brother's gym. About fifteen minutes away at this time of night. He smiled. His *chica bonita* had picked a good meeting place. Isolated. Past closing time. They would be alone.

He would leave the *mafiosos de poca monta* to their watch while he met with their prey. If the *estupido* gangsters were still there when he returned, he would dispatch them.

If they followed him, he would do it sooner.

CHAPTER ELEVEN

A STRANGE CALM settled over Charlie as she rested her head against the back of the timeworn leather chair in her brother's office. She was glad she'd asked Luc to come over. The thought of having him there made her feel a little more secure.

Her brother had gone home and with only the nightlights on in the rest of the building, the boxing ring stood out as if under a soft spotlight…like a noir scene from some old black and white movie. The place was eerily quiet and Charlie could almost hear the sounds of her memories coming to life; her father's laughter as he sparred with the teenaged boys he'd mentored, her own giggles when teased by Uncle Emilio and her Poppy whenever she came to the gym with her daddy. Strong men.

It was her father's legacy, the gym. And no matter how long he'd been gone, she would never stop missing him. Someday there would be justice. She would find out who was responsible for his murder. If she knew nothing else, she knew there was no such thing as a perfect crime. She just had to find the evidence. Finding Mia Powers was no different.

Lights flared outside. Headlights. Luc. He hadn't hesitated for a second when she asked him to meet her. He was decisive. Confident. A man who knew what he wanted.

She went to the window, peeked through the slots in the blinds, and watched Luc exit a Lexus CT200h. A nice ride, one of the least likely to be stolen, according to an article she'd read recently. Not that he would care. The car was probably part of his job with the senator.

On her way to the door, she flipped on the light, and then glanced in the peephole to again confirm it was Luc. She opened the deadbolt and two other locks, leaving on the safety chain until she had a visual.

"I'm glad you could make it," she said, sliding the chain. She still had some reservations about how wise it was to invite him here and no idea if she could even trust the man. He had to have been well vetted by the senator, so she wasn't worried about that. What worried her was that he might report back everything she said and did to the senator. But she had to trust someone, and for some reason, she wanted to trust Luc.

"When a beautiful woman calls, I am always available."

"I'm sure you are." She cringed at the blatant flattery and motioned him inside her brother's office.

"I have spent many hours in a place like this," he said, moving toward the ring instead of the office. "I believe you have, too. No?" He turned to look at her, his dark eyes drinking her in. He looked taller tonight and wore more casual clothes, faded jeans and a black V-neck T-shirt under a leather jacket. Edgy. Sexy.

"When I was growing up, I did. After that, not as much. Mostly only the time necessary to learn basic self-defense. Enough to take care of myself." Except for the thugs waiting outside the casino. Epic fail.

"I could teach you some skills that would greatly enhance what you already know." His eyes twinkled as he spoke, the subtext in his smooth tone obvious. One side of his mouth lifted in a smile.

"Thank you for the generous offer." The only skills

she needed right now were self-restraint and the willpower to keep her from doing something she'd regret later. "But I have more urgent things on my mind."

He nodded. "The offer is open should you change your mind." His smile grew a little wider. "I say it sincerely. Much of self-defense involves the brain. Staying focused. At the casino when those men attacked, you let your emotions get in the way."

"Something I already know. And you're right. I could use more training. Just not now."

He leaned against the edge of the mat, a position she'd seen her father take so many times. She hauled in a breath. Yeah, focus. She needed to focus. "Tell me, what did you do before becoming a bodyguard that taught you these many skills?"

He turned. "Do you really want to know?"

"I really want to know."

He schooled his face into a mock dark expression. "I am a trained assassin working for a secret government agency—so secret even the highest government agencies do not know it exists."

She sighed heavily. Gave him a look. "Are you never serious?"

His eyes darkened. He stepped closer, within inches, and with two fingers lifted her chin so she looked directly into her eyes. "I am very serious, *querida.* I was a Captain in the United States Army 75th Ranger Regiment, Special Troops Battalion. As a sniper, my job was to kill people."

Charlie's breath caught. Whether from his revelation or his nearness, she wasn't sure. But it was all she needed to know.

"Let's go into my brother's office. I have something to show you."

Her heart beat triple time as she plunked down on

one of the client chairs and motioned him to the other.

Luc glanced at her brother's street art she'd framed to decorate the office.

"My brother's work. He's very creative. Would you like something to drink?"

He leaned back. "I would like to sit here and drink in your loveliness, but I don't believe it is what you meant."

She snorted. "Really? Drink in my loveliness?" Where did this guy come from? "I think your English teacher missed the mark in some areas."

Luc frowned. "I believe my mother, while poor, was a very good teacher. She loved the arts, and the opera and wanted to instill the same in me. She loved the beauty in life, language in particular and taught me both English and Spanish. Although, to my regret, she was never able to experience the beautiful things she told me about before she died."

Charlie's cheeks warmed and suddenly feeling two inches tall, she wanted to slither from the room. "I'm sorry. The death of a parent is an awful thing. Perhaps she believed passing along her knowledge to you was a way to keep the beauty she believed in alive."

His frown turned quizzical, eyes softening as he looked at her. Then the edges of his lips turned up just a little. "I like that. You are a perceptive woman. Beautiful and perceptive. It is a very nice combination."

Beautiful. The gangly too-tall kid who'd been called giraffe, the loner who'd been bullied in school because she was the daughter of a murderer—was beautiful. And perceptive. She took a deep breath. This was getting way too deep for her. Pretty soon she'd be babbling about everything her dad taught her...and her mother and her Mexican grandmother and a whole lot of stuff not relevant in any way to why he was there.

But his sharing something so intimate gave her more

confidence in what her intuition had been telling her. She could trust him.

"There's water and some power drinks in the kitchen." She tipped her head in that direction.

He raised his hands. "Thank you, I'm good."

Yeah. He was. She shifted position and reached for her messenger bag on the desk. "So, let's talk about why I wanted to meet with you."

His expression turned serious. This time for real.

"As you know, Senator Hawker is my client, and he's told me you are trustworthy, and I can count on you to give me any help I might need on his case."

"Yes. This is true."

"Well, I've had some things happen that make me think my investigation is ruffling someone's feathers."

He gave her a blank stare.

"Ruffling feathers…it's a cliché. A metaphor for making someone take notice."

He grinned. "You are making me ruffle the feathers, too, *bonita*. I don't wonder that you might be making many others take notice, too."

"It's not meant in a good way. What I meant is…whatever I'm doing in the investigation now has someone following me, and they smashed the window on my car earlier tonight."

Luc reached out and touched her cheek. "Are you okay? Did they hurt you?"

"I'm fine. But I wanted to talk to you about those men, the ones who are following me. I need to know what they want and why they want it."

"How do you know they want something?"

"They smashed my window and stole Mia Powers' duffle bag from the passenger seat in my car. I'd already taken out everything except the work clothes and shoes, so unless they're into kinky stripper clothes, they didn't get what they want. Given their intensity,

I'm sure they'll try again."

"And you want me to protect you."

"No, I want you to find out who they are and what they want."

"That will be easy. They have been following you for a while."

"What?"

"I saw them at the casino when you were playing cards."

"Aha. So you *were* following me the night at the casino."

"No, I was watching you play poker, and not so wisely, I might add. I could teach you a few things there, too."

She waved her hand. "I'm sorry. This is serious business for me," she said, needing to get to the point.

Apparently getting the hint to cease and desist, he said, "Yes, they are the same two men I observed at the gentlemen's club and then again tonight outside your apartment."

"At my apartment?"

He nodded. "And you are wondering now what I was doing there." He smiled.

She hadn't gotten that far yet, but it was a good question.

CHAPTER TWELVE

"I WAS THERE because you are representing the senator, and I wanted to know why they were following you," Luc said. "They could be the men who tried to rob you and stole your handbag at the casino. They may want to harm you if they believe you can identify them."

Charlie could identify them easily. And all her personal information was in her purse. They knew where she lived. But they wouldn't have had any reason to steal the duffle bag.

"Or maybe you are a closet gambler and owe some bad people lots of money and they want to collect."

Only the first part was true. The last part was in the past. And she didn't need her former gambling excesses to become public knowledge. It could cost her the job she so desperately needed. As it was, she was pretty much on probation. Known for doing whatever was necessary to get the job done, Douglas had strongly suggested when he hired her that she follow company policy and procedure. That included not bending the rules to suit her needs.

"Or someone knows I'm looking for Mia Powers to clear the senator's name, and they're worried I'll find something to incriminate them in the process."

"Or, you already did?"

The duffle bag. "Right." And Charlie still couldn't decide if she should tell him what she'd found inside. One minute she trusted him, and the next her guard came up. Bottom line, she didn't know enough about him. Trust went only so far with a virtual stranger.

She shook her head. "There were also some old photographs in the bag and a necklace. I'm thinking the necklace was a gift from someone." She shifted in her chair to face him. "It's a very expensive necklace."

"Then we should find out who gave her the necklace. It seems strange she would leave a valuable piece of jewelry in a bag and never return to get it."

"Unless something bad happened to her and she was unable to do it." And the more she thought about it, and remembered Mrs. Powers saying how mean the senator was and how her daughter had lost contact with the family, the more Charlie wondered. Abusers weren't recognizable at a glance. Anything was possible. She didn't want to think it, but Mrs. Powers could be right that something bad *had* happened to her daughter.

"You contacted all of her friends and family members?"

"I was never able to track down anyone else. Mrs. Powers said Bunny Archer, whose real name is Adeline Archer, and Mia had been friends for years." Charlie then told Luc what Mrs. Powers had said about Mia's old college friend Jean-Luc Fontainebleau calling a short time before Mia disappeared. "I think these two people may be key in figuring out what might've happened to Mia."

"Why would they not come forward?"

"I don't know. Bunny came into some money. Maybe she was paid off."

"And Fontainebleau?"

"I haven't had time to locate him."

"If you'd like me to, I can find out why the two men were following you and make them stop."

"Just like that?"

Luc's eyes locked with hers. "Yes. Just like that."

Seeing the hard certainty in his eyes raised goosebumps on her arms. He sounded like a fixer for the Detroit mafia. Working in the prosecutor's office, she'd been a part of two cases that involved the mob she was very familiar with the structure and major players.

He tipped his head, as if asking her permission.

She shook off the ridiculous comparison. He wanted to help. Wanted to protect her. "Okay. But I want to come along."

He arched a brow. "It could be dangerous."

In more than one way, she was sure. "It's an opportunity for me to learn something, and with all your skills, you can protect me. Right?"

He grinned. "If you do not get in the way."

"Alright." Charlie couldn't help grinning, then lifted her clenched hand for a fist bump.

She got a blank stare.

Yeah. Okay. "High Five!"

Luc had suggested Charlie drive home, and he would follow shortly behind. That way if the men were still at her apartment, they would be watching her and not him. He could get the drop on them and…and what? She had no idea what he'd do then. Call the police? Threaten them?

It wasn't what she'd envisioned when she'd said she wanted to go along, but Luc was an experienced bodyguard, expert in a lot of areas, apparently, and she was eager to learn.

If she had to work for RB&B for a while longer, she could at least make it interesting. Investigating was far more interesting than their usual corporate lawyer stuff, which most of the time was dull paperwork.

When they arrived at her Midtown condo on Woodward and Watson, Charlie, following Luc's instructions, parked and proceeded to go to her unit. Luc would circle around and text her if he saw anything. If he saw no one and confirmed no one was watching, he would come to her apartment and they would talk about what to do next.

Charlie didn't see a single person driving into the garage. She parked, then rode the elevator to the second floor and, at the apartment door, she was digging in her purse for the key when she heard a noise behind her.

She swung around, her pulse racing. Her neighbor, Barry Daniel from one apartment down and across the hall, waved. A sense of relief washed over her. Damn, she was jumpy.

"Hey, Charlie," Barry said. "How's everything?"

"So far, so good," she lied. "How about you? Did the promotion come through?"

He walked over. "Yeah, it did. Hey, some men were here looking for you earlier."

"Men? How many? What did they look like?"

"Two. They looked like the guys in the movie, *Men in Black*."

She laughed. "Okay. Any other distinguishing features? Did they say anything?"

"No, they were just there at your door when I came home. I went into my apartment and when I looked out again, they were gone."

"So they were dressed like the guys in the movie?"

"Yeah. Black suits, black hats, sunglasses. One white guy, one black. I could see they had bulges under their jackets, like they were armed. It was kinda weird. I thought they might be going to a costume party or something and had the wrong place."

"Maybe. I have no idea who they were. Did you hear them talking at all?"

"Nope. I thought about asking if I could help, but like I said, they were gone when I came out to ask."

"Okay, Thanks for telling me, Barry. I appreciate it."

Barry returned to his apartment, and she texted Luc about the two men. If they were outside, he'd probably seen them by now. She got out her key and went inside, leaving the door cracked a hair so she could see to flip the light switch on the far wall.

It was dark, but the blinds were still open and the street lights gave off enough light for her to see a little bit. She reached for the switch. A hand clamped over her mouth. She screamed, but all that came out was a muffled squawk. Her eyes adjusting to the dark, she glanced around.

Stuff was strewn everywhere. Couch cushions sliced to shreds. Drawers hanging open, cabinet doors ajar. Her desk dumped upside down.

"Where is it," a deep voice, hoarse and raspy, commanded. "What did you do with the hard drive?"

"Nothing in the bedroom," another voice called out.

Two. There were two men, and Luc wouldn't see them because they weren't outside, they were inside. Her heart crashed against her ribs. Emotions, Luc had said. Don't let emotions get in the way.

"Where is it, bitch?" the guy behind her growled out again, his arm around her neck...squeezing.

Gasping, she shook her head. How the hell did the idiot expect an answer when he had his hand over her mouth and was choking her? He was directly behind her and she slid her foot over to tell where his was. Her self-defense training kicking in, she stomped on his instep, dropped down, turned and while he was screaming about his foot, kicked him in the *cojones*.

Within seconds another guy burst from the

bedroom. One of the men Barry described. Black suit, black hat, black man...and a gun pointed directly at her. Just then the front door burst open and crashed against the inside wall. Luc charged inside, fists and feet flying and shouting something in Spanish. Her eyes blurred. The man let go and shoved her forward toward Luc. She stumbled, and Luc caught her at the same time he threw a punch, connecting with the guy's jaw. She scurried out of the way amid a flurry of fists and feet, all three men swinging and kicking. She heard the crunch of knuckles against bone, an *omphh* when someone got punched in the stomach. It was two against one and she needed to help. Backing up to find something to use as a weapon, she bumped into something behind her. Someone. Someone big. She swung around.

"What the hell...?"

Shit. Barry. She pushed her neighbor out of the way. "Get out of here before you get hurt."

She grabbed his shirt and dragged him into the hallway and as she did, a man crashed into the door, shutting it with a bang. She looked at Barry. "Do you own a gun?"

His eyes rounded like dinner plates. He shook his head? "No. But I have a baseball bat."

"Good. Can you get it for me?"

While Barry went off to get his bat, she got out her phone to call the police. Barely a second passed when Barry returned with not one, but two bats. He gave her one and held the other one, the look on his face like a little kid eager to go out and play. "Let's go," he said.

Okay. Why not? He could probably strike harder than she could anyway. "Just the men in black. Not the other guy."

He nodded.

Crap...they were all in black. "Not the one in the leather jacket."

Barry nodded again. She tipped her head toward the door and they inched forward. Bats raised and at the ready, Charlie reached to turn the knob, but Barry's leg shot out next to her and kicked the door open.

Expecting the same scene, she charged inside, then did a dead stop. The lights were on. The men were nowhere to be seen. And the window to the fire escape was open.

They were gone. All of them.

She looked at Barry and shrugged.

He smiled. "I guess we scared them away."

Ten minutes later, she'd put the condo back together. Sort of. Barry had been so excited, he'd been hard to get rid of, but he'd finally left when she told him she was doing secret government work, and he couldn't be there. She'd thanked him profusely and said she'd make sure the people she worked for would know of his bravery. A few minutes later, Luc returned.

"Same guys?" She leaned against the closed door, adrenaline still rocketing through her veins.

Luc nodded. "They had a car waiting, so I didn't go after them. I checked to make sure there weren't any others."

"And?"

"They were alone. I'm sure they will return. I will take care of them then. For good."

She didn't know what he meant by "for good," but right now, she didn't care. She was so pumped, she could fly to the moon on her own power. She motioned him farther inside and to sit. He didn't and she couldn't, instead she paced from one side of the small living room to the other.

"They want the hard drive I found in the duffle bag."

He was quiet for a moment, brows coming together. "Why don't you give it to them?"

She stopped in front of him. "Why would I do that?"

"Why not? It means nothing to you."

Although he was taller, wearing heels, she looked him in the eyes. "No, it doesn't. But it means something to Mia Powers. And she's not here to get it."

"What difference does it make? You don't know her. And if it goes away, your client does not have to worry about it anymore."

Charlie ran a hand through her hair, his closeness disturbing. "If the hard drive has the senator's personal financial records on it, they will prove the allegations against him to be false."

"You do not know what's on it?"

"Not yet." Landon had promised to find a couple hackers and if he couldn't, she was sure Max knew a few, too.

"What if the information proves otherwise?" His warm breath fanned her face, his eyes still locked with hers.

Her breathing deepened. She moistened her lips. "I-I'll cross that bridge when I get there. Right now I'm more concerned about a woman who's disappeared and no one is doing anything to find out what happened to her."

"So you're going to do it."

She nodded. "I am. And I *will* find out."

Luc smiled, and pupils dilating, his head dipped toward hers in a soft kiss. Gentle.

Her body melted into his. She returned his kisses, softly, fiercely, the adrenaline of danger like lightning in her veins. All the sparring, all the innuendoes, and the danger...everything seemed to come together to create this one passionate moment in time.

Still kissing her, he backed her against the wall. He

trailed a finger down the front of her shirt, softly cupped her breasts. "*Precioso*," he murmured.

She moaned. A lot.

Then slowly, painstakingly slowly, he unbuttoned her shirt. "I want to make love to you, my beautiful Charlize."

Her fingers flew over the buttons on his shirt, then went to his belt buckle. She was so ready she might come without him even entering her… and *he* wanted to go slow? Pure torture. She kissed him hard and fierce. She touched him, unbuttoned his jeans, slid her hand inside and there he was. Hard as stone and ready.

He groaned, sucked air through his teeth, then lifted her arms and placed them around his neck. "Not yet," He said. "I am but a man…and weak sometimes, too."

Like she cared? She raised one leg to get closer, pressing into him to release the pressure that had been building since the moment they'd met.

"It is much better if we take some time, *bonita*. I can give you much pleasure." He pulled up her skirt and slid one hand slowly up her leg, his fingers playing around the edges of her bikini panties, barely touching, and yet, she was on fire.

She pushed against him. "I can't wait."

His hand slipped under her panties, he dipped one finger inside, then stroked ever so slowly. One stroke and she couldn't stop the release that began like a long-burning stick of dynamite, then exploded in wave after wave of exquisite pleasure. She moaned. Or screamed. She wasn't sure, and the orgasm seemed to go on forever and ever. When it subsided, he touched her again.

"That was just the beginning, *querida*."

CHAPTER THIRTEEN

"THE NORTHWEST LOWER Peninsula," Senator Hawker blathered on from his easy chair about his hunting trip, explaining the finer points of the kill, as if Luc were a child and had no idea what hunting was all about.

Luc suppressed a grin. He knew more about hunting and killing than any human should know. And he'd already mapped out the entire area where the senator and his old buddy would be meeting next week. He'd walked the area on the computer numerous times. The only problems would be the things he could not control. Like the weather. And spur of the moment decisions the *estupido* senator might make.

They were at one of the senator's five homes, this one being on one of Detroit's finest golf courses at Oakland Hills Country Club in Bloomfield Hills, on the north side. When the senator wasn't carrying out his fantasies with as many women as he could, he was on the golf course. And once in a while he was in Washington.

So many idiots getting paid for doing nothing. As for golf, it was an old man's game. Luc was used to being active and just thinking about a game like golf made him itchy.

But he was a patient man when he needed to be. And he still needed the intel on the vice president's arrival, including the stats on how many secret service agents he would have to contend with. Luc's plan had to be carried out to the minutest detail, or it wasn't going to work.

Any tiny little thing could throw off everything. A scenario he was intimately familiar with when taking out dictators or high-profile heads of state. Details were of the utmost importance.

He'd hacked into the senator's personal computer files, but hadn't found anything on the vice president's arrival or where they would meet. That was one thing the senator *didn't* blather on about. He suspected even the senator didn't know. So far, the intel he'd obtained said they would meet at the senator's cabin on Torch Lake, in northwest Michigan, and after a night, they would travel to the hunt from there. "Will you want me to help the vice president with anything when he arrives?"

"He will have more than adequate coverage, but I may need you to procure some entertainment for him while he's here." The senator looked at Luc over the top of his reading glasses. "If you know what I mean."

"That will be easy. Just tell me what type of entertainment the vice president desires, and I will do my best to get him exactly what he wants," Luc said, though he already knew what Spector liked. Very young girls, too young to know what Spector might do to them. Young girls who didn't get pregnant and if one did, like his mother, he'd beat her within an inch of her life and leave her permanently scarred, both body and soul.

Yes, he knew exactly what the senator liked and would get it. Unfortunately for the VP, he would not be able to enjoy it.

"Excellent. We may need some extra entertainment for the vice president's entourage to keep them busy as well."

"It's done. Perhaps the entertainment will be around later when I am through with work."

The senator broke into a hearty laugh. "I pegged you for the smooth Casanova type. All you Latin guys seem to have some extra testosterone or hormones or something. "What about the attorney. Have you banged her yet?"

Instant heat rushed through Luc's veins. He clenched his hands. He could snap the *pendjo's* neck in an instant. The senator was fortunate Luc had to focus on his goal. He would not do anything that would interfere. "The attorney is not my type, Senator."

"Hah!" Hawker laughed again. "Just as well. A block of ice seems warm compared to her. Did you find out anything? I haven't heard from her or Douglas in days."

"I have nothing to report. Perhaps they don't have anything new to report, either."

"Good. That's what I want to hear. All she needs to do is get me off the hook. When she does, I'll give you a bonus."

"You are too kind, Senator."

Luc was not concerned with personal wealth or politics, but he'd lived in poverty and saw first-hand the broken lives of those who suffered at the hands of the rich and powerful…like pompous politicians who siphoned the peoples' money and left a trail of broken souls in their wake.

"I like to reward people who do a good job, Luc. It's how I maintain a loyal, dedicated staff."

Luc nodded, tamping down the urge to strangle the son of a bitch right now and put him out of his misery.

The senator scratched his crotch. "Why don't you take a couple days off? I'm going to hunker down at home to get some things done before I have to return to Washington."

He'd learned quickly that hunkering down didn't mean business, or alone time. It meant a procession of prostitutes would be brought in for whatever fetish the senator wanted taken care of at the moment.

"Just be available if I need you."

Luc picked up a photograph on the narrow table behind the sofa where the senator sat. A photograph of the senator, his late wife, and his young son. The woman was wearing a necklace and an exquisite diamond ring large enough to feed Luc's village in Mexico for months.

"I'm at your service, Senator."

"She called while you were in the meeting." A new face at the reception desk handed Charlie a note on the phone call.

"Where's January?" Charlie placed the small package on the reception desk, a present for January, who'd gone above and beyond getting information for Charlie on Jean-Luc Fontainebleau.

The receptionist, who looked about twelve, shrugged and said, "I don't know. Something important at home, I heard."

January had a little girl and was separated from her husband in another state, and who Charlie suspected of being an abuser. January hadn't told her that, but from everything Charlie could gather from their conversations, it was fairly obvious. She'd handled many spousal abuse cases when working pro bono while in law school and recognized the signs.

"Did she say anything? Whether it's urgent or not?" Her mother had called twice two nights ago when Charlie was with Luc. No way was she going to stop to answer her phone. She smiled inside at the memory.

Her heartbeat quickened just thinking about it.

"No." The temp cleared her throat. "But she sounded annoyed that you weren't available."

Crap. Her mom was going to be even more annoyed since the work was flowing and she'd have to return the call later. Not only that, she had a lunch date with Landon in—she glanced at the clock—fifteen minutes. Damn. There weren't enough hours in the day.

But that would all change once she managed to open her own firm. She would make sure things ran like a fine-tuned instrument. First of all, she wouldn't take on more cases than she could handle since it would be just her until she could afford to hire another attorney.

"Okay. Thanks. I have an outside appointment, so I'll be gone for an hour or so," Charlie said. She'd call her mom after lunch. She had no idea what her mom might be calling about. She never did. The woman was as unpredictable as a flash flood. What she did know was that it was never urgent, even though her mom thought so.

Ten minutes later, Charlie entered Elwood's diner located directly behind and below the Comerica Park scoreboard. The restaurant had been around a long time, but relocated when the new ballpark was constructed.

Landon was already there, a beer in front of him and a server hanging on his every word.

"Hey, just in time," Landon said as Charlie sat across from him in the booth.

The server's giddy expression faded, apparently thinking Charlie was his date.

Landon pinned the girl with his bluer than blue eyes. "My sister is here just in time to order." He tipped his head toward Charlie. The girl glanced her way. "You ready to order, Ma'm?

Ma'm? "Uhm, sure." Just give me a second to glance at the menu."

"Would you like something to drink?"

"Water is fine." When the server left, Charlie said, "Hey, twice in one week, good brother, sister contact."

Her brother laughed, took a sip of beer. "Did you find out what was on the hard drive?"

"No. Did you have any luck finding someone who can do it?"

"Not yet. T.J., the one guy I know is out of the country. I've got a call in to another guy, but I don't know him very well. Don't know how trustworthy he is. I think I'd rather wait for T.J. to get back."

She agreed. Trust was huge. It could cost her job if she messed this up. The server returned and Charlie still hadn't looked at the menu. "Just give me the same thing as my brother," she said, then turned back to Landon. "Okay, so what's going on with Mom?"

"Sheesh." Landon rolled his eyes to the ceiling. "What isn't? Did you know she's talking about going on a dating site? It's been over twenty years and now she suddenly decides to date?" He raised his hands in the air. "How crazy is that."

Charlie laughed. "That's it? I thought it was something important."

"It is." Landon drew back. "Who knows who these guys are, what they want."

"Well, I think she's old enough to figure that out, and she's still young enough to want something other than sitting in a rocking chair until she dies."

"Landon's eyes narrowed. "You think it's okay?"

Charlie lifted her chin. "Hell, yeah. I told her to do it. I told her I'll help her write a profile, but since she never asked, I didn't think she'd actually do it."

"You told her to do it. Damn. I should have known." He sighed. "Geezus, Charlie. What were you thinking?"

"It was either that or get her a puppy to keep her

busy, and she's allergic."

"Well, so much for her undying love for dad."

"She still loves him." Too much for him being gone for over twenty years. "But now that she's retired, I think she needs something else in her life."

"Maybe. But it doesn't have to be a dating site. She should find someone in church or someplace else. Not where all she'll find is scammers, players and married dudes."

"Church? Really?" She gave him a look. "She'll be okay." He was right though, there were plenty of players out there. She'd found more than one. "In her age group, how bad can it be? Even if she just has coffee with someone, she's doing something other than calling me with every thought she has."

Landon pressed his lips together. Shrugged. "There is that. Hey, maybe you should take your own advice. When was the last time you had a da—"

"Uh-uh." Charlie wagged a finger. "No, no, no. You are not turning this back on me. Besides, I'm fine in that area." She smiled. "More than fine."

"Jean-Luc Fontainebleau?" Charlie said when someone picked up the phone. She put the phone on speaker so she could talk and page through the records on her computer monitor at the same time. At last, someone who might have talked to Mia before she disappeared.

"My name is Charlize Street. I'm an attorney and—"

"Not interested."

"Mia," she said quickly before he could hang up. "I'm calling about Mia Powers."

"Well, you've called the wrong person. I haven't talked to Mia in years."

Click.

She pulled away, stared at the phone. The prick hung up. She was about to punch redial, but stopped. No. Too easy to hang up, again. She had his address.

Thirty-five minutes later she was standing on Jean-Luc's doorstep in Ferndale, a Detroit suburb along the Woodward corridor where the annual Dream Cruise took place. A green and white '55 Chevy was parked in the drive. She smiled. She and Jean-Luc had something in common. They liked vintage vehicles.

Once a year, she got her dad's old Mercedes out of the storage building at the gym and participated with all the other car geeks who cruised their restored vehicles for a solid week along Woodward Avenue. The old 450SL had been her father's most prized possession and, as her friends kept telling her, it could be worth enough money to help her fund her business.

Her friends were right. The car in its pristine condition and few miles was worth enough to start her business, but to her, the vehicle was worth more than money. It was a symbol of her father's life…showing he'd been here and wasn't forgotten. She'd never sell it.

And now, the car, she'd decided when at the gym with her brother, was the perfect place to hide the hard drive until she found a trustworthy hacker to get into it and see what was on it.

She rang the bell, then knocked on the door for good measure. Someone peeked through the blinds in the front window. Then the door opened part way and a slightly built man about her same height scowled at her from inside.

"Jean-Luc Fontainebleau?"

He pointed to a NO SOLICITORS sign in the bottom corner of the window. "I'm guessing you can't read," he snapped, then moved to close the door.

"I'm here about Mia Powers," she blurted and stuck

her foot in the opening so he couldn't slam the door in her face. "I really need to speak with you for just a minute. It's extremely important."

"You're the one who called, aren't you?" He gave her a good once-over, then tsked and crossed his arms. "You're a persistent bitch, aren't you."

"I can be and in my profession, that's a good thing."

"Well, it's not in this case. Mia and I haven't seen each other since college when she dumped our friendship to party with the real boys. I will always hate her for that."

Seeing some photos on a table in the entry, Charlie squinted to bring them into focus. The photos were of Jean-Luc and another man, arm in arm. Apparently, what Mrs. Powers had meant when she said Jean-Luc was 'different.'

Charlie didn't give a rat's ass how different he was. He could be purple for all she cared. "I don't blame you. I would be angry, too. But all I really want to know is when you last spoke with her."

One eye twitched ever so slightly. He looked away

Aha. Her question had touched a nerve.

"I haven't spoken to her since college. And I really don't have to tell you anything. You're wasting my time."

"Her mother said you called and wanted to talk with Mia. Why would you call if you hate her so much?"

His mouth pinched. "I called her mother's number because someone called me from that number. I didn't know who it was and if I had, I wouldn't have returned the call."

"Did you ever talk to her? To Mia, I mean."

"No. And I wouldn't talk to that witch even if she transformed into Magic Mike."

He slammed the door in her face.

Jerk. She stood there for a moment. His over-the-top

reaction to a simple question was telling. It had to be at least five years since his college days with Mia. How could someone carry a grudge for so many years? *A woman scorned*, came to mind. Only in this case, it was a guy. She couldn't help wonder what he might do if he did see Mia.

On her way to the car, she glanced back at the house, then pulled out her phone. What if Jean-Luc did talk to Mia… and they had a fight… and things went south. She thumbed through her phone files for the information she'd saved on Adeline Archer. *Bunny Archer*. They'd all been friends in college. Bunny might know if Jean-Luc was the kind of person who could hurt someone.

All she had to do was find Bunny. Then again, maybe Jean-Luc was the one who paid Bunny to move and keep quiet.

And maybe her imagination was running amuck.

Still…

She needed to talk to Bunny.

CHAPTER FOURTEEN

AT HER DESK at home, Charlie logged on to the internet and Google, then put in Adeline Archer's name again. She was pretty good at using legal databases, skip tracing software, and public records to track down people.

She'd even done a search on Luc after they'd made love. Oddly, she'd found nothing. Not one shred of evidence the man even existed. That would normally be a red flag, but he'd been in the military and the intensive vetting the senator had probably done told her he had to be okay. Still, there was something about him that niggled at her. Her good sense said stay away, but her body didn't agree.

They'd made love all night long, and Luc was everything he'd said he was in the bedroom. And more. The high adrenaline rush of danger had been working overtime, and they both knew it. She had no regrets...and no need for it to be anything more than that. But it was a one-night-stand she would not forget.

A message popped up on her computer. Max sending her information. She began reading... Jean-Luc's home was in his parents' name. They were both dead. Died of carbon monoxide poisoning last year. Hmm. Curious, she clicked on the link Max had sent for their obits in the *Detroit Free Press*.

Reading their combined obituary, she discovered Jean-Luc's parents owned another property in northern Michigan in Antrim County. A cabin? One of the photos Mia had in her possession had been taken at a cabin. She'd thought the photo had been taken at the senator's place, but what if it was taken at Jean-Luc's? If it was, then he'd been lying about not seeing Mia.

Maybe Jean-Luc *was* responsible for Mia's disappearance?

Charlie shoved a hand through her hair. God, she needed a trim. Not first on her list these days, especially since it was easy to simply pull it back into a pony tail. As long as she was presentable at the firm, she was okay. She clicked down, scanning for pertinent information, some tiny little thing could change everything. Mia had been the senator's mistress and his personal finance manager. He'd said the last time he'd seen her was at his cabin.

Her fingers clicked over the keyboard to Google Earth and northern Michigan. The senator's cabin was located on Torch Lake. Jean-Luc's parents' cabin was on a smaller body of water, Intermediate Lake. The properties weren't too far apart. Ten miles, maybe.

Two things she needed to do. Find out what was on the hard drive, and make a visit to the senator's cabin. Mia had kept the photos for a reason. If she'd been at the senator's cabin right before she disappeared, there had to be evidence somewhere.

Except her brother's car that she was using would never make it that far, and her own was still minus a window. But there *was* another option.

She braced a foot on the floor and pushed off, sending her chair wheels cruising over the oak hardwood floor to the breakfast bar. Her blood pumping, she grabbed her phone and punched in Luc's number. "Do you know if the senator is going to his cabin any time soon?" she asked when Luc answered.

There was a slight pause, then, "No. I happen to know he will be very busy at his home for the next couple of days."

"And you?"

"He does not need me during this time."

"Perfect. How would you like to take me for a ride?"

"A wonderful idea, *bonita*." His smooth bass voice literally purred. "I am ready to be of service any time."

Geez. "Does everything have to be sexual with you?"

"Is that bad?"

Hell, no. But… "You said I had to focus. That's what I'm doing, and it isn't going to help if you keep—"

"Where would you like to go, Miss Street? I am a very good chauffer."

"I have no doubt. Northern Michigan. The senator's cabin. It's about four hours away. And you cannot tell anyone. Including the senator."

"Done. Would you like me to procure a key?"

"Excellent."

"When do we leave?"

"Tomorrow morning. Very early. We can drive up and come back in the same day."

It was perfect, Luc mused as he rode the elevator to the parking garage under his apartment building. He could keep track of the lovely Charlize and do his own research at the same time.

His *chica bonita* would be very surprised if she knew he was staying directly across the street from her. She would be mad. *Muy enojado*. He smiled. The combination of fiery Latino and tempestuous Irish lass was deliciously compelling.

She was beautiful when she was mad at him. And beautiful when she was happy. He couldn't remember ever being so smitten. He might even be falling in love with her.

A terrible thing for both of them. His profession was not conducive to anything other than brief encounters that required nothing from him. Attachments, emotions, made you vulnerable and could be used against you. Emotions made you make mistakes.

Mistakes could be deadly.

He pulled into the circular drive in front of Charlie's apartment building and parked in the lot on the north side. She didn't say what the trip was about, but he was sure it had to do with her new interest in finding out what happened to the senator's mistress. He was happy to oblige. He had planned on scoping out the area before the vice president arrived, so this little trip worked very well into his own plans. He'd dressed casual, wearing lightweight, yet sturdy shoes in case he decided to go for a walk in the woods.

From the maps he'd studied, the senator's large tract of property backed up to state land, which was where the senator and the vice president would be hunting. He'd studied the area on every type of topographical map available, but there was nothing better than an on-site visit.

If he'd had enough notice, he would have done it before taking the job with the senator, but when opportunity arises, one must act.

And everything was moving along perfectly.

He smiled at how easy it had been to get rid of the two men who'd been following Charlie. He'd roughed them up a little and paid them more than they'd been paid to follow her. In exchange they'd told him they were after a stolen hard drive. And it was in Charlie's possession.

But they were not the men at the casino. Those men were professionals. They had been seated where no one could approach unseen and yet with a view of the entire gaming area. They'd been drinking, but not really drinking. And they were watching him, too.

The two he'd paid off were like kids dressed up for Halloween. And, unfortunately, they did not know who'd sent them. Their payment had been orchestrated by a third party through the internet and PayPal. He had the information and when he had time, he would hack into the accounts and see if he could find out more. He'd thought the senator had hired the goons, but since he'd learned of the senator's dealings with Tony Carlozzi, the underboss for the mafia, he couldn't be sure. If Hawker was dealing with Frankie Falcone, the grand puba of the Detroit mafia, also known as The Partnership, the senator was treading on very dangerous ground.

Under other circumstances, Luc would have simply ended the two stooges, but too many bodies in a short period of time around the senator and his attorney would bring more people on the scene. Law enforcement officers and FBI. Maybe others, since the vice president would be here next week. Best not to draw attention. Luc didn't need a side show. He needed a normal, calm environment.

He needed some quiet time with his sweet and sexy *chiquita*.

He needed time to be a normal person. If even for just a day.

CHAPTER FIFTEEN

CHARLIE TOLD LUC about her suspicions. She didn't tell him she thought a cabin in the woods backing onto state land would be a good place to hide a body. She didn't really want to think it herself, but since she hadn't been able to find Bunny Archer to learn more about Mia, she hoped to find some kind of clue about what happened to her. What she really needed to know was why Mia had stolen the hard drive in the first place…and what was on it that someone wanted it bad enough to smash her window and break into her apartment.

Her brother had found a hacker friend who'd tried again to get into the hard drive, but even he couldn't get past the password stage. He was as much a novice as she was. There had to be hackers out there who could do it, but with corruption in the city government and in the police department being uncovered at every turn, she didn't know who she could trust. Until she had more information, she wasn't turning the hard drive over to anyone. Not even her boss.

Charlie entertained the idea, more than once, that someone had killed Mia to keep the hard drive from surfacing. Although she didn't like thinking it, her first thought was the senator since it was his information that was missing. But the senator was a well-connected man. He could easily have information on a lot of people who might not want information about them revealed.

She glanced at Luc, looking confident behind the wheel of the black Lincoln Navigator. Sexy in his black V-necked tee, casual jeans, and glove-soft leather jacket.

"So, why the different car?' she asked, again.

"It keeps us off the radar."

"Whose radar? I thought you said those men weren't a problem anymore."

"Correct. But you have something someone wants. That person will hire others to take their place."

"Well, they will be disappointed, then, because I don't have it."

Luc glanced over, his smile tight. "Where did you put it, *bonita*?"

Something in his manner, the way he'd hesitated just the tiniest bit when she said she didn't have it seemed...off. "It's...safely hidden. I didn't think carrying it around was a good idea."

"Very smart. I hope you found a better place to leave it than in your apartment. That would be the first place anyone would look."

Her skin prickled. She angled her head at him. If he wanted to know, why didn't he just ask? "Really? Gee. I never would have thought of that."

"I'm sorry, *mi amor*. I did not intend to hurt your feelings."

Charlie stiffened. Crossed her arms. Good grief. How paranoid was she? She was the one who'd asked Luc to drive her up here. But now, her gut was saying something wasn't right.

"My *feelings* are not hurt. And I am not your love or your sweetheart or your pretty girl or darling or whatever other condescending name you decide to use next. My name is Charlize or Charlie, or Ms. Street. I even answer to ma'am or hey, you. So please knock off the misogynistic euphemisms and use the real thing."

The smile on Luc's face wilted. A hurt look flashed in his eyes, then a millisecond later, his expression went to stone. "I will remember, Ms. Street. I apologize for offending you. I was under the impression telling a woman she's beautiful is a good thing, but I should know better than anyone that all cultures are not the same."

Heat filled Charlie's chest and radiated up her throat. Fuck. She was an idiot. And she had no idea what had set her off like some shrew. Dammit. She took a deep calming breath…like she did to calm her nerves before speaking to a courtroom full of people, most of them thinking her client was guilty as hell.

"No. I'm sorry. I'm the one who needs to apologize. I don't know what happened there." Other than the fact that he inferred she was stupid, and he was trying to manipulate her. "I'm usually more in control." She was always more in control when it came to her job. But she'd let her guard down. She'd forgotten she was on a job. "I seriously do not know what prompted that."

Yeah. Luc *was* smooth. A player. And she had drunk the Kool-Aid and believed him…trusted him. When all he'd wanted was to get information from her for the senator. Charlie sighed, leaned her head against the seat and closed her eyes. Why did it even matter?

It mattered because…because she…liked him. A lot.

They were both quiet for a long time, the rhythmic hum of the tires along the highway the only sound. The early morning sun winked in and out of the towering Norway pines, the forest getting thicker with each mile northward. They were getting close. She opened the window to feel the cool air and breathe in the scent of pine needles and moist, dark earth. "Have you ever gone camping?"

He glanced over. "Like in a tent?"

She nodded. "My family used to drive up here in the summer, to one of the lakes. We couldn't afford to stay in a motel or cabin, but we had a small tent that we slept in. All four of us...like a family sleepover. When we first arrived at the lake, we'd all strip down and run into the water, even before setting up the tent."

He gave her a questioning glance.

"Oh." She laughed. "We wore swimsuits under our clothes. Then, after we put up the tent, we'd catch fish and cook them over a campfire."

Grinning, Luc turned, his expression thoughtful. "No. Outside of the military, I never had the opportunity to go camping. There weren't any forests near where I lived. But it sounds like a wonderful family time. How old were you?"

"Young. Before my father..." She glanced out the window. "Have you heard about—"

"Some."

"It's not true, you know. He wasn't guilty. Someone framed him and then had him killed in prison."

She saw a muscle under Luc's eye twitch a little.

"Do you know who was behind it?"

He didn't question it or ask her why she believed her father wasn't guilty. That was a first. "I have ideas, but no way to prove anything. If he'd had a good attorney..." She cleared her throat. "A good attorney could have found a way, or at least put up a good defense argument. But my father didn't have money for any attorney, and according to everything I've read about the case, the public defender was a skittish kid fresh out of law school. He should never have been assigned to such a high-profile murder case. So..."

"So?" He prompted.

Charlie sighed. "I've spent years trying to find evidence to exonerate him."

Luc reached over. Placed his hand on hers. "You will. Criminals always leave something behind."

"Yes. I firmly believe that. And I will find it. Someday. But, my obsession, as my mother calls it, sort of took over my life. When I lost my job because of it, I vowed to knuckle down and save money so I could do what I started out to do."

"Work for a big law firm with important clients like the senator?"

"No. Helping others who may end up in prison because they have no money for adequate representation."

"Ah, yes," Luc said. "Justice is always a little more just for those with money."

"Exactly. That's the reason I went to law school. The reason I want to start my own firm. And when I have enough money saved, I will do it. I need to stay focused on my goal."

"And finding your father's murderer?"

She smiled. "I will. However long it takes. Justice will prevail."

Luc glanced at the GPS screen, then he turned to her and bobbed his head. "Now I understand. That is why you fought so fiercely when you were attacked at the casino."

"It was enough money to bid on a building I know is coming up for auction. If I add a little more, I can renovate and have my own place. At Street Law, half of the cases will be pro bono and the other half will pay the bills."

"Street Law. It has a nice ring to it. You should do that."

"I will. It's just a matter of time."

The car bumped her against the door as Luc turned

off the highway and onto a gravel road. "How far away are we?" She glanced at the GPS screen. Saw a huge lake and some other smaller ones. The big lake, she knew was Torch Lake, and above and a little east was an elongated body of water connecting some smaller lakes.

"Almost there. The senator's cabin is here." He pointed to one side of the bigger lake.

"And Kid Rock's and Michael Moore's."

Luc raised a brow.

"A rock star and a documentary film maker. A few famous people have homes on this lake. In fact, one of Kid Rock's songs mention the lake, which is famous for its sandbar and the hundreds of boats and thousands of people who congregate there on the fourth of July to celebrate and watch fireworks."

"Thousands of people. It doesn't sound like something I would want to attend."

"Mmm. Me either," she said, studying the map on the screen. She trailed her finger along a smaller road. If they went straight up and through Bellaire, they would be very close to Jean-Luc's cabin on Intermediate Lake.

"What are you thinking?"

"Would you mind if we took a little detour before going to the senator's cabin?"

CHAPTER SIXTEEN

THERE WAS A VEHICLE ahead in the long driveway. Luc coasted to a stop, far enough away not to be seen.

"Jean-Luc's car," Charlie said. "I saw the same car at his house yesterday. That's really strange."

"Why? It's his cabin, isn't it?"

"Yes, but why would he rush up here right after I was at his house asking questions about Mia? Maybe my suspicions are right?"

"About what?"

"That there's a body buried in the woods somewhere around here."

Luc had considered the possibility for a while now, but not about this Jean-Luc person. The senator was as much a sociopath as many criminals. If the senator had killed his wife, he would have no compulsion about getting rid of a mistress who'd stolen his records. The woman had probably thought the hard drive was her home-free card, but instead it was her death warrant.

But that was not why Luc was there. He had one mission. Get a mental map of the land, then...take out *El Diablo*.

"Park over there where he can't see us," Charlie said, motioning to a small clearing at the side of the road. "I want to talk to him for a minute, but it's probably best if you wait here."

He pulled over to where his line of sight on the cabin was clear, but he would still be hidden from view.

Charlie exited and headed to the door.

Fontainebleau's cabin sat on a large wooded piece of property with no other cabins visible in any direction. The property, except in front of the cabin facing the lake, was filled with amazingly tall pine trees. White pines and red pines, he'd read during his research of the area. The white pine was the state tree, distinguished by its crowning canopy and tallness, towering over all the other trees. The tallest one recorded reached 210 feet.

The rest of the landscape included some maple and oak, birch, and a few silvery leafed trees, creating a colorful surround of persimmon, ochre, deep reds, golds and varying tints of green. The warm air was redolent with the scent of pine needles and dry leaves. Refreshing. With many places an assassin could use for cover.

If he lived in this state, this would be his favorite time of the year, he decided. The air was cool and clean, and with the sunlight dancing off the water like diamonds, the setting was almost magical. If he had a second choice on where to live, a place like this might be very nice. Away from people. Away from the hypocrisy and petty rivalry that too many people wanting too many things invariably created.

But the ocean was home...his small house in *Puerto Peñasco* on the Sea of Cortez...that was where his heart went when he thought about home. Not the hellhole of Tijuana where he'd grown up. Or his many places of business.

Getting out of the vehicle to stretch his legs, he saw Charlie at the door talking to a young man. Light brownish hair, puny, and the man was waving his hands and shaking his head. And then the little shit slammed the door in Charlie's face. She stood there for a moment, still as a statue.

One side of Luc's mouth tipped in a smile. His feisty *chica bonita* was not going to like that at all.

When she charged back to the car, arms pumping by her sides, hands balled into fists, he could practically see the steam rising from her body. Pretty much not the time to be making jokes, he concluded. And not the time to be sympathetic.

As difficult as it was, this was the time for Luc Cabrera to keep his mouth shut.

"Asshole," she said stomping toward their vehicle. "What is the problem with him? He's way too angry. A five-year-old snub wouldn't make someone go off the deep end like that, would it? I mean, unless there's some other reason...why would he be so rude? And why would he rush right up here after I'd just been at his house yesterday?"

Luc shrugged, sensing it was still not time to talk. Let her get it all out first, so he was not the recipient.

"I think he's nervous as hell that I'm going to find out something. That's what I think."

She was wearing a long, wool turtleneck sweater, dark jeans and camel tan boots that matched the sweater. A soft scarf hung around her neck untied and flapping in a crisp breeze from the lake. Her lusty hair blew back, free in the wind, fire flashing in her eyes.

Luc slid into the driver's seat.

Charlie walked over to a tree and kicked it. Spouted a few words damning the *bastardo* to hell and a few other exquisite curses. He grinned.

Waiting until she was inside to start the car, he looked over. "Ready?"

A scowl fixed on her pretty face. She crossed her arms. "Ready."

The senator's cabin was the complete opposite of Jean-Luc's rustic century old model with its patched and weathered siding and pitted natural stone fireplace marching up the outside of the two storied structure. Charlie had craned to look far enough inside Jean-Luc's to see the fireplace and determine if it was the one in Mia's photograph. That's all she'd wanted to do.

If it was the same one, she would know if Jean-Luc had lied about seeing Mia Powers before she went missing.

And she'd failed. But she wouldn't this time. They would go inside the senator's cabin and if it wasn't the same fireplace, she would know the photo wasn't taken there. Jean-Luc's place had to be it.

The senator's egregiously opulent cabin sprawled out before them. Even though it was built out of logs, it was three stories high, with more than one massive fireplace climbing the exterior. Redwood decks of all sizes abounded from walls of glass on the first floor, second and third.

There were no cars visible, but a seven-car garage sat off to the right. Probably for the expensive vehicles of wealthy guests attending indulgent parties the senator allegedly gave for his cronies. And funded by the state. Her opinion of the senator was in rapid decline.

"The senator likes antique cars and keeps a few in the garages I've heard," Luc said, as he opened the driver's door and stepped from the vehicle.

"Good for him." She'd been so focused on finding the senator's missing records and discovering what happened to Mia Powers, it was easy to forget the senator was her client and it was her job to make sure he was cleared of any wrongdoing. But her doubts were rising.

What she really needed to do was stop looking for

problems outside of the case, find someone to open the hard drive, and prove the senator was not a crook. Someone who wouldn't turn the senator in if it turned out he *was* a crook. God. Could she even do that?

Her stomach roiled at the thought. Every ethical nerve in her body was telling her the opposite of what she personally wanted to do. Ethically, confidentiality was king and, even if she found the senator was as crooked as Lombard Street in San Francisco, she could not breach confidentiality. Not even if she took herself off the case.

Her personal values and morals didn't matter. If she stopped searching right now, she wouldn't have to think about any of it.

Glancing at Luc walking toward the entry, she exhaled a long breath. She could talk to herself all day long and not come up with the right answer for her client. Because she had to know. She couldn't ignore it. Whatever the outcome, she had find out what happened to Mia.

"Wait for me, Luc," she called, jogging through the fallen leaves to catch up. "Massive, isn't it?"

"Disgusting."

She smiled. "I couldn't have said it better."

His hand went to the small of her back when they reached the steps, guiding her to go first. Her breath caught at his warm touch. The man was so sexy he felt on fire. "Did you..." she cleared her throat. "Did you get a key?"

He pulled a key from his pocket. "Voila."

"Perfect."

She watched while Luc used the key. The wide double doors opened into a massive two-story foyer, where a chandelier made of deer antlers hung halfway down. To her right was a large room that looked like a lounge of some kind...or a reception area in a hotel.

Through the floor to ceiling windows, the strangely still turquoise waters of Torch Lake glistened like a sheet of clean glass.

"I've never seen a land-locked body of water that color before," Luc said, laying a hand on her shoulder.

"And look at this fireplace," she said quickly moving out from under his touch. As much as she wanted to trust him, she didn't trust herself. And no matter how much she wanted to pretend otherwise, all good sense would disappear the second she let her hormones take over.

"That's not the fireplace in the photograph," she said, walking over. She pulled the photo from her messenger bag. "I guess I'll have to check all the rooms with fireplaces to see if it could be one of the others."

"The photo could have been taken at some other person's home. Another friend."

"The photo is fairly recent, and her mother said she didn't have any friends, not once she began working for the senator. Her mother said he even kept her from seeing her family."

Luc nodded. "You go ahead. I see a library, and I love books."

CHAPTER SEVENTEEN

A WIDE SCREEN laptop sat on top of a seven-foot long mahogany desk in the senator's library, which was stocked better than the libraries Luc had frequented as a kid. When he wasn't stealing money from tourists and food from the markets.

He sat at the senator's desk and clicked on the laptop. Within seconds the monitor screen lit up. Password protected. He'd watched the senator put in his password on his home computer so many times he had the motions memorized. He closed his eyes and visualized, made his fingers follow the same pattern. Bingo! So easy.

He pulled up the files. Not so easy. Most were encrypted with a code he knew would take him a while to crack. He pulled out an empty flash drive and began downloading. In the meantime, he pulled up the available files and subfiles. Seeing one series of files listed as 50 WTLYL, he clicked and opened it.

Not much surprised Luc anymore. Most humans, he'd discovered could be as cruel as they could be kind. It was all a matter of perspective and the depth of their need. And as he scrolled through his boss's research, it appeared the good senator had a deep and abiding need to see someone dead.

Luc found numerous searches about undetectable

ways to murder someone, and drugs that cannot be identified easily in the body. The picture was becoming clearer and clearer.

Hawker had not only killed his wife, he was probably responsible for his mistress's disappearance as well. But Luc couldn't let Charlie know. Not yet. If she went to the police with the information, it could ruin his plans for the vice president. He needed time. And to do it, he had to ensure the hard drive she had in her possession didn't go anywhere.

Upstairs, Charlie went from one room to the other. So far she'd checked three fireplaces in three different bedrooms. And got *nada*. The fireplace in the photo of Mia was made of fieldstone, not flagstone or brick or marble as in the senator's house.

She'd been through four bedrooms already and still hadn't found the master bedroom. The next one she entered was smaller and looking around, her heart stalled. Sunlight shone through blinds half closed making everything in the room shadowed in stripes. On the bed, a family of teddy bears lay as if someone had played with them recently. Legos were strewn on a small desk, painted blue and white. Everything in the room was blue and white.

Zack's room. Mia's mother had said the senator's little boy's name was Zack, and she vaguely remembered it from when the news media had been covering the boy's disappearance. Her heart went out to Hawker again. How could anyone not feel for a man whose beautiful son had been kidnapped? She had nothing but sympathy for him where his little boy was concerned.

Charlie heard a noise downstairs. A door slammed.

Luc? Or someone else? She rushed through one last room. The master bedroom. Marble fireplace. Not the one. That was all she needed to know. On the way out, she saw a photo on the dresser, similar to one she'd seen on the news. Next to the photo in a small crystal bowl was a set of rings. Wedding rings.

Her throat went dry. Geez, had the senator taken his wife's rings off after she was dead? Wouldn't she have been buried wearing them? Ugh.

Just as she was going to leave, Charlie took a closer look at the photo. The necklace. Mrs. Hawker was wearing a necklace exactly like the one Mia had in her duffle. The same questions she'd had before rolled over in her mind. How had Mia come to have such an obviously expensive piece of jewelry? Had Mia stolen the necklace? Or had the senator given it to her? More importantly, why would she leave it in the bag when it was worth so much money?

Or... had she left the necklace as a clue if something happened to her? So many questions, Charlie's mind literally reeled with it. She shook it off and dashed down the stairs. "Luc," she called out. She checked the library. Not there.

Then she saw him on the front deck, just standing there, staring out at the water. She went out to join him.

"Nature is the ultimate turn-on," Luc said, looking at her over his shoulder. "It makes me want to make love to you outside with the sun shining down on us, the crisp air stimulating our naked bodies."

Whoa. "I think you've been hitting the tequila in the senator's bar."

"No. But I did find a note on the senator's computer. Only it's not to his wife or to his mistress."

Charlie clenched her jaw. The senator was her client and because he'd been through a lot with his wife's death and his son's disappearance, she'd been sympathetic, had even thought he was different than other politicians. But apparently not. He might be worse. Corrupt to the core. The sleazy creep was sleeping with other women besides his wife and his mistress. "Bastard."

Luc tilted his head toward her. "Is that any way to speak of your client?"

"I work for him. I don't have to like him."

"I know the feeling."

The worst thing was that the senator had been dishonest with her...his attorney. Above all, guilty or not, a client had to be honest with his attorney. It was impossible to put together an adequate defense if she was going to get surprised by things the client didn't tell her. Not telling her something was the same as lying.

She turned away. Looked at the lake. She'd been duped. Played by a fucking politician. Who had a boat the size of a small cruise ship moored at the dock below. She shook her head. The senator was doing very well on his government salary.

"I'm going to take a look at the boat."

Luc nodded. "Let's go."

Together they walked down the slight hill to the dock where the boat was moored.

"I saw a photo where the senator's wife was wearing a necklace exactly like the one Mia had in her bag," Charlie said.

"You are very observant, *bonita*. You would make an excellent spy for the government."

"Really, Luc? We're talking serious stuff here."

"And I am serious." He grinned.

She ignored him and went back to piecing together her thoughts. "The senator could have given the necklace to Mia and she didn't like it... or maybe she was embarrassed because she knew it had belonged to his dead wife." Charlie didn't believe it, but it was one scenario, and she had to look at all of them. "I also saw his wife's wedding rings on the dresser. She was wearing them when she died. I remember it from the medical examiner's photos."

"You saw the photos?" Luc frowned.

"Max, my investigator, dug them up."

"Interesting. Are you thinking Senator Hawker killed his wife now?"

"I know that's a big leap. And there's no real evidence. But there's plenty of proof that he's a creep and a lying, cold-hearted snake."

Reaching the dock, Luc waited, then took Charlie's hand and helped her on to the senator's yacht.

"This is amazing. A freaking house on the water," she said peering inside the cabin. "There's a whole kitchen down here." She took a few steps down to go inside. "You coming?"

He shook his head. "I thought I saw something up near the cabin. Probably just an animal, a bear, maybe. I'll wait here just in case."

"Very funny. There are no bears around here."

"That's not what my research tells me."

Charlie stepped further inside the cabin. Women's underwear and cosmetics were strewn everywhere. "It looks like there's been an orgy or something in here." She couldn't picture the squishy bodied senator taking part in an orgy. She took out her cell phone and took some photos.

In the bathroom, she glanced in the medicine cabinet. Pills. Several bottles of Flunitrazepam, also called Rohypnol and Roofies. The date-rape drug, which was illegal and could get someone a lengthy prison sentence. Despicable was the only word she could think of to describe someone who'd got those lengths to have sex. And why? What would be the benefit? It had to be like having sex with a dead body.

She clicked off some more photos, then opened a small linen closet, glanced at the shelves, and the built-in waste container at the bottom. She was about to shut the closet door when she saw a small piece of a something white protruding from the waste container.

She tugged and out came a plastic bag closed with a twist-tie. She took off the tie and holding the bag a little away from her face, opened it and glanced inside. Hypodermic needles and some empty bottles. Was the senator a diabetic? A junkie? She picked up one of the bottles. The name wasn't anyone she recognized. A visitor on his yacht, maybe. She read the drug name. Succinylcholine.

The name of the drug sounded familiar. Probably from an episode of *Forensic Files*. She quickly Googled the drug on her phone, moving around to get reception inside the boat. When the page finally came up, her eyes glued to the screen. The medication metabolized instantly in the blood and was virtually undetectable. When injected, it would cause paralysis and asphyxiation.

Immediately she thought of the senator's wife. But she had drowned in the bathtub after taking other drugs and alcohol. Could Hawker have... no. That was really a stretch.

She glanced at the date. Over a year old. She clicked off some more photos. There could be an explanation, and she was sure the senator had one. She put the bag back in the waste basket exactly like it had been when she found it.

Doubts tightening her stomach, Charlie climbed the stairs to the yacht's deck. "Luc?"

She glanced around, not seeing a single sign of him. Sunlight sparkled off the water so bright she raised one hand, shielding her eyes from the glare.

There he was, crouching near the bow, peering in the direction of the cabin.

"Luc?" she repeated. "I think we have to–"

Luc shot to his feet, faster than seemed possible. Then he was running straight at her. He crashed into her, sending her careening to the deck.

She hit hard. He came down harder. Smack on top of her.

Pop! Pop! Pop!

A sharp pain stabbed the back of her head where she'd hit the yacht's deck.

Pop! Pop! Pop!

Was that sound what she thought it was? It came from behind…at the shore. "Gunshots?"

Still on top of her, his face inches from hers, Luc raised an eyebrow. "You are very observant, *querida*. Yes. Someone is shooting at us."

She pushed at him to move. He didn't budge. "Be serious, Luc. Whoever it is, he could kill us! Even if it's just a security guard thinking we're trespassing, we won't get to explain if we're dead."

"*Si*. But it is not *a* security guard. I have counted two of them. And they certainly could kill us, but for the fact that I am prepared." He reached between their bodies and pulled out a very dangerous looking handgun.

"Put that away." She pushed again to get him off her, but he barely moved to the side. "We just need to explain why we're—"

"We do not have time, and those men will not listen."

"You don't know that."

"I know security guards do not shoot first and ask questions later."

Her heart stalled. He was an experienced bodyguard. He had to judge situations all the time. She glanced at his gun. She had little experience with guns, not shooting them. She heard gunshots all the time in some of the neighborhoods where she'd grown up, and she'd gone target shooting with Alan once, but that was it. It made sense that Luc would carry, of course. He was a bodyguard. But just seeing the lethal weapon in his hand sent a chill up her spine.

He reached down and produced another gun from a holster fastened to his calf. "I need you to do something for me."

Charlie stared at the second pistol. "You can't be thinking what I think you are thinking."

His gaze swept over her. "Probably not." He grinned at her, as if this was all a game.

"I don't know how to shoot."

"Ahh, yes. But you are a quick study. I have learned that about you, my sweet Charlize."

"A quick study? You're going to risk our lives on me being a quick study?"

"I told you before that I have been known to enjoy gambling."

"You're gambling? On me?" Charlie held up a hand. Her fingers shook so badly, they appeared to be twitching. "That doesn't seem like a good bet about now."

"It is the surest bet I've made in a long time." He kissed her. The touch was brief, but still managed to be intimate and deep.

Deep enough that she felt the intensity all the way to her toes. After a long second, he moved over and to a sitting position.

"Sit up."

She raised herself so she was sitting next to him.

Luc placed the second gun into her hand, snugging the handle tightly into the web between thumb and first finger. He molded her fingers around it, her index finger pointing along the side. He did the same with her left hand. He moved to a crouch and motioned for her to do the same and then follow him to the yacht's side. Once there, he positioned her hands, so she was pointing the weapon in the direction of the house.

She could barely see over the edge of the boat. Her heart pounded triple-time.

"Now I will count to three, and when I hit three, I need you to start squeezing the trigger."

"Oh, no." She shook her head. "I'm *not* going to shoot at another person. And even if I could, I wouldn't be able to hit anything while crouching down here like this." And not with the way she was shaking, either.

"I don't require you to hit anything or anyone. Especially not me." He gave her a wink.

"How can you be so calm?"

"It is easier to function when calm. Much tougher to be frantic, no?"

He was right. Again.

Charlie pulled in a deep breath, pushed the panic from her mind, forced herself to think. He wanted her to fire the gun, not shoot anyone. Okay, she got it. "You want me to cover you."

Luc chuckled. "You can do it, yes?"

"I can." She sure *hoped* she could. "And what are you going to do?"

"Find out who is trying to kill us."

Kill us. He was going to risk his life— "Please don't…"

He scowled.

Yeah, stupid request. "Well, don't get hurt, okay?"

The scowl disappeared. His eyes softened as he looked at her. "I will try not to, *bonita.*"

"Good. I wouldn't like that."

"Nice to hear. Now I want you to shoot ten times in the direction of the house, then run downstairs, hide in the cabin, and wait until my return. Understand?"

"Yes, yes." She looked at him, fear in her eyes.

He reached up, gently touched her cheek. "It will not help to return only to find you hurt."

She nodded. "I wouldn't like that either."

"So are you ready?"

Charlie scooped in another lungful of air. "Ready."

"One."

Charlie focused on the feel of the gun in her hand, blocked out every other emotion, especially the way her body trembled. She gritted her teeth. Mentally steadied her body from spine to fingertips. Miraculously, all her senses drew to one focal point, her body a block of steel determination.

"Two."

His pistol at the ready, he coiled his body, prepared to spring.

"Three."

Charlie squeezed the trigger, again and again, her world exploding in her hand.

CHAPTER EIGHTEEN

LUC LEAPED OVER the yacht's edge. He was already running when he hit the pier, the sound of his footfalls on the boards masked by Charlie's fire.

When he told her she was a sure bet, he hadn't been lying. As frightened as she was, she'd pulled herself together and followed his instructions letter for letter.

She was something, his beautiful Charlize.

He reached shore, ducked behind the boat house before she was finished with her ten shots. Perfect timing. Now she needed only to take the next part of his directions to heart and hide in the yacht. This is what worried him most.

Luc pulled out his phone and fired off a verbal text. HIDE NOW, QUERIDA. IF ANYONE BOARDS THE BOAT. SHOOT HIM.

In the next split second, he shoved pleasant thoughts of Charlize from his mind, pocketed his phone, held his HK5 compact tactical pistol at the ready, and focused on the *pendejos* trying to kill them.

Only rank amateurs could be so incompetent.

Luc hadn't seen them get into position while he was searching the yacht, or after he'd left the library. That could only mean they had already been in position when he and Charlie had crossed from the lake house to the yacht. During that stroll and later on deck, they'd been open targets. Any competent sniper would have taken them out before they knew he was there.

Many times, Luc had lived through others trying to kill him. If someone knew who he was, they never would have sent these two *payasos*. That could only mean they were here for Charlize.

And for that, they would be very sorry.

He moved to the corner of the boathouse, listening to the stillness beyond. The first round of sniper fire had come from a high trajectory to the east. From here, that would place the sniper on a rocky hill overlooking the lake.

Luc dipped a hand in his pocket and pulled out a small scope that had proved useful on many occasions. He peered through, studying the brush and crags of the hillside. Sure enough, something glinted in the sun. A closer look, and he discerned the barrel of a rifle, its aim directed to the yacht.

So there was *número uno*.

The fire from número *dos*, on the other hand, had come from the cabin's west side. And due to the flat, rich man's lawn reaching to the lake, this one would be more difficult to deal with. If Luc approached directly, the shooter would have an open view of his target, and Luc would be left staring into the bright sun.

But if he was able to turn the tables? Circle around from behind?

Keeping close to the boathouse wall, Luc sized up the lake house. While the street façade had the look of a rustic mansion, the lake side was a series of balconies arranged like stair steps all the way to the slate roof.

The architect couldn't have made it more convenient.

Luc moved low and fast along the sculpted landscaping at the edge of the yard, reaching the house in seconds. And a moment later, he was pulling himself up to the first balcony and slinging his leg over the rail.

It felt good to move. To do something. As much as he enjoyed being around the fiery Charlize, he had been relegated to riding in cars and watching her question people for far too long. The last time he'd had a good workout was making love to her, and that had not happened nearly often enough to sate him.

He moved to the next balcony, only half a story above the first. Then to the next and the next. Finally he pulled himself onto the hot slate shingles.

Slate was bad in the rain, slick as ice. And in the heat, it was like climbing on the surface of a frying pan.

He moved low, quickly scampering over the apex and ducking to the shadowed side, the rubber soles of his shoes already feeling a little gummy from the heat, his palms uncomfortably scorched. Once on the other side of the roof, he paused, listening.

No sound, not from the man he hoped was still below or the man on the hill.

So far, so good.

He moved to the edge of the roof and peered over. His target was still there, almost directly below a second story balcony.

Luc's luck was intact.

The man was wearing some kind of khaki-colored fatigues, but the long hair at the nape of his neck made it clear he wasn't military. Not military. Not an experienced sniper. From this angle, Luc couldn't see his rifle, although he knew it was there.

Not that it mattered. The *cabrón* wouldn't have a chance to use it.

From here, Luc could easily put a round in the back of the guy's skull, but that would only tip off *número uno* and wouldn't reveal who the duo worked for.

Luc crouched on the edge of the roof. Grasping a section of slate where there was no rain gutter, he rolled over the edge, using just the strength in his hands and arms to hold his one-hundred and seventy-five pounds. He let his body hang down then dropped catlike to the second story deck, absorbing the impact with his knees.

One more drop.

The next one would have to be quick, but to make it work, Luc would have to land almost on top of his target. Unfortunately he was too far away. He spotted a small ledge where one of the logs stuck out a little further than the others. A rich man's version of rustic. But for his purposes, just what he needed.

He would move out on the far log, drop from there, and be in the perfect position to take his man. The logs on the siding were round with nothing to grab, but some had larger spaces between. If he could get a grip just long enough to hold him until he could put his foot on the lower ledge… without making a sound… he could do it. He would literally be hanging by his fingernails. But it was the only way to take the man without resorting to gunfire.

All in a day's work.

He grabbed the bottom rail of the deck and slowly lowered himself to where he could get a grip into the sliver of space between the logs. His fingers slipped even as he grabbed hold. He dangled, found the ledge with his foot and steadied himself just long enough, then dropped to the ground directly behind the man carrying an OTs-23 Drotik, a Russian made machine pistol with a 14 round mag.

Russian. Interesting.

The soft *thunk* of Luc's feet as they touched ground made the man turn.

"Surprise, *pendejo*." Luc landed a jab to his target's larynx, his hand moving fast as a rattlesnake.

The Russian grabbed his throat, eyes widening with the realization he couldn't breathe. He pivoted to get away, but Luc reached his right arm around the target's neck and grabbed the man's left arm below his biceps. He slapped his left palm against the back of the guy's head and pushed down, compressing the carotid arteries in his neck.

The Russian flailed, hands clawing at Luc's arm, but Luc held strong, waiting until he felt the *sicario's* body go slack.

He released the man's throat. Holding him up on his feet, he waited until his head bobbed, blood flowing back to his brain, regaining consciousness.

"Who sent you?"

"Fuck off," the man mumbled.

Luc tightened his choke hold again, and again the man struggled, then dipped into unconsciousness.

When Luc lightened up, letting the man stir back to awareness, Luc growled into his ear again. "I'm warning you. I can choke you over and over until I get answers, but will you manage to keep coming back? Now answer my question. Who sent you?"

The man grunted, then threw his head back.

The rear of his skull clipped Luc in the jaw, and motes of light sprinkled the air in front of Luc. A roar rising in his ears, Luc bore down again, hiking his elbow hard against the man's throat, shoving his head forward.

This time, the man didn't wake up.

Luc released him with a sharp twist. "Es*tú*pido," he said, then let the body fall to the ground. He would return to dispose of the body after he had a chat with *número dos*.

With only one man to worry about, his travel was faster and more direct. Crouching, he moved across the north side of the house, climbed the hill, and zagged into the brush and trees so he was directly in line with the other *asesino*. He approached from behind.

*Número do*s was wearing the same type of khaki

fatigues and wielding a Russian military sniper rifle, an old self-loading Dragunov that had a range of no more than 350 meters.

He'd been right. Amateurs. And probably not Russians at all. Most of the Russian mafia in Detroit was aligned with La Cosa Nostra and other groups and gangs, and they were far from amateur.

Not eager to have another bruise marring his face when he had a pretty lady waiting for him, Luc moved up behind the man, silent as a soft breeze, and leveled the HK on his head. "Put the rifle down."

The man tensed, and for a second, Luc thought he might spin around and try to be a hero.

Dead hero.

Instead, he seemed to rethink his stupidity and set the rifle down on the rocks.

"Hands on your head."

The man complied.

"Now, I just need to warn you that your friend didn't want to talk to me, and he is now dead. Unlike you, I have killed many men. Most deserved it, and some I just did for fun. But others, those who gave me what I wanted, they lived to be old men. So this is my question for you. Who sent you here to kill Charlie Street?"

Charlie jumped at the gunshot. Just one. Cold, stark panic shot up her spine. She'd gone into the cabin and locked the door as Luc had said. But now she didn't know what was going on.

She punched 911 on her phone again. Same as before. No cell reception.

But that gunshot... Luc could be hurt. Or worse. What would she do if someone broke down the door? She picked up the gun again and bracing against the wall, held it out in front of her. What if the gun was empty? What if she'd shot more than the ten rounds Luc had told her and used up all the ammunition? She was trapped like a rat, her body shaking so hard she could rock the boat.

Waiting, a million thoughts flashed through her head. All she'd wanted to do was help a client, but it turned out her client could be guilty of even more than he'd allegedly done. A few pill bottles weren't proof of anything, but they might be enough to justify starting a real homicide investigation. If the senator *had* killed his wife, there was a good possibility Mia might have also have met Mrs. Hawker's fate.

And if *she* died before telling anyone, no one would know about any of it.

If she lived, she would be bound by client confidentiality.

No matter how she sliced it, Senator Hawker was going to get away with murder.

Maybe even hers and Luc's.

Dread infused her. Luc could be out there injured or dead.

Charlie thumbed 911 on her phone again. Nothing. No signal. She couldn't sit here all day waiting for someone to kill her. If she took the gun with her, she could go find Luc. God, she prayed he was okay.

A sound outside. Footsteps on the dock. Her heart rocketed to her throat. She clenched the gun tighter. If someone came in, she'd just pull. And keep pulling. But her hand shook so hard she could barely hold the gun up. *Go away! Please, please, please go away.* She didn't want to shoot anyone. But if she had to…

"Charlie. It's Luc. Can you open the door?"

She bolted from the floor, her numb fingers fumbled with the lock. Luc pushed the door open at the same time as she pulled. She rushed into his arms. "You're okay. Thank, God, you're okay."

He held her close, rubbed her shoulders, then tipped

her face up and kissed the tears from her cheeks. "They're gone."

"Gone?"

He nodded. "We need to leave, too."

"You said they...how many were there? Why were they shooting at us?"

"We must go." He steered her toward the door. "They could return so we need to leave."

She climbed the stairs, dizzy from hyperventilating and imagining Luc injured or dead. He kept his arm firmly around her, directing her to the dock and up the stairs toward the car.

"Are you okay? Blood. She saw blood on his shirt. "Are you hurt?"

"I'm fine. I wounded one of them, but they may have friends."

"We need to call someone."

"In due time, *bonita*. In due time."

It took Charlie a good five miles to calm herself and even then, it was only on the surface. Her nerves still jangled under her skin. Now, after a few more miles, they were almost to the town of Bellaire, a short distance from Jean-Luc's cabin. It was getting dark and she needed to pee. "I really need to use a restroom."

"Okay, let's see what we can do."

Luc seemed so totally calm it was hard to imagine he'd done anything even remotely dangerous. He looked as if he could've been lounging on a couch reading a book all day. And she had to look like hell.

As they drove down the main street in Bellaire, she motioned to a building on their right with a sign that read, Short's Brewing Company. "What about that place?"

"As good as any," Luc said, then pulled in front and parked near an area with empty tables.

It was October and getting late in day. She wouldn't want to sit outside to eat either. "Looks like they have food, let's grab a bite to eat, too."

He glanced down, pulled his jacket closed covering the blood on his shirt. "Okay, I'm hungry and thirsty."

Going inside, the place wasn't very full, nothing like she would imagine in the summer. All the small tourist towns filled to capacity when the weather was hot. Even though there were only a dozen or so people there, all eyes seemed upon them. A hostess directed them to a booth near the front window and Charlie immediately asked where the restroom was located.

Once inside the room with shiny steel sinks shaped like beer kegs, she splashed water on her face and glanced at herself in the mirror. She'd been crying and hadn't even realized it until Luc had held her and kissed her tears away.

He thought she was fine now, only she wasn't. Her nerves vibrated under her skin, questions kept circling in her brain. Some of them about Luc. He seemed so unaffected by it all. So…cold.

Except where she was concerned. He'd cared about her feelings when they'd made love. He was, in fact, the warmest and most giving man she'd ever been intimate with.

She finished in the rest room and made her way back to the booth, her senses still reeling. Luc had already ordered a flight of beer and motioned for her to sit and have some. "I took the liberty."

"I-I don't know about the beer. I haven't eaten anything all day."

"Then we should eat."

Although the menu was varied and she knew she needed to eat, she shook her head. "Too many choices.

I can't think. Anything is fine." God, someone had actually been shooting at them. Shooting to kill.

The waitress appeared for their order. Luc glanced at her to go first. She shrugged.

He ordered a large pizza with everything on it, then looked at her again. "Pizza is always good, yes?"

She nodded, and the server scurried off. Arms folded across her chest, she leaned forward, touching the table in the booth. "I've never shot a gun before."

Luc bobbed his head and tasted one of the small glasses of beer. "Umm. That one is good. Try it." He handed her the glass. "It is called—" he looked at the list "—Soft Parade."

His eyes stayed on her as she took a sip. He was right. It was good. Ice cold and slightly fruity tasting.

"You did very well, today," he said. "You will be fine once you stop thinking about it."

"That's the thing. I can't. Now I'm thinking I need to learn how to use a gun. I mean really use it. The right way. And beef up my self-defense skills."

He frowned.

"I live in Detroit. I was attacked at the casino and they stole my money. Two men smashed my car window and stole Mia's bag while I was sitting inside the vehicle. Two men were following me and broke into my apartment. I'm in a business where I deal with criminals all the time. I think I need to learn how to defend myself, both physically and with a weapon."

He grinned. "Give the lady a taste of power, and look at what happens."

Her nerves bunched. "It's not a joke. A gun is not power. Power lies between here and here." She touched one of his ears and then the other. "But personal safety is another thing. Self-protection. Can you teach me how to use a gun?"

"Under the circumstances, I don't know how long I

will be working for the senator, but I will while I can. After that, I know someone who can teach you. He is an excellent weapons instructor and has experience training people in self-defense."

"Is that what he does for a living?"

"No. He is a lawyer."

Odd resume. "In Detroit?"

"No, but I understand he will be there soon."

Their conversation floated around Charlie like something apart from herself. Words were coming out of her mouth, but all she really heard was that Luc may not be around once his employment with the senator ended. Which could be soon if Luc reported what they found at the senator's cabin.

Since she'd taken the photos on the senator's property, where she happened to be without the senator's permission, her photos wouldn't be admissible evidence in any court. But the senator's files would be since there were already charges pending. What she had to do was find someone to hack into the senator's hard drive to see what was there. Then she could decide what to do.

"Does your friend happen to have brilliant computer skills?"

Luc's eyes lit up. "Not that I know of. But I am intimate friends with someone who does."

"Don't tell me." She held up her hands. "You?"

CHAPTER NINETEEN

UNBELIEVABLE. WAS THERE a skill Luc didn't possess? One, she decided as they settled into the car after polishing off the pizza and the small flight of beer. It wasn't much beer between them, but along with the ebbing adrenaline, she could feel the effects.

Intuition. That was the skill Luc didn't possess. Or if he did, he was ignoring it. Because right now, hers was telling her something wasn't right with the exchanges she'd had with Jean-Luc. It had been niggling at her since their very first meeting. His anger seemed so disproportionate relative to what was supposed to have happened between him and Mia. There had to be something else going on. Maybe he really did know what happened to Mia and, like Bunny, someone had paid him off?

Okay, she didn't know that for sure about Bunny, but, given the intel they had, it seemed logical. "Can we take a little detour?" she asked once they were on the road.

"Again?"

"I want to talk to Jean-Luc."

"Really?" Luc's brows knitted together in the middle. "He doesn't want to talk to you."

"It's important. Trust me. Something isn't right."

He shrugged. "As the lady wishes." He played with

the GPS and returned to the address for Jean-Luc's property. A mile later, he turned off onto the gravel road leading to Jean-Luc's place. A car passed them going the other direction. "Wait," she said. "That was him. He's leaving."

Luc jammed the brakes. She jerked forward, and his arm slapped across her chest.

"Sorry. Automatic response."

"Yes, when one has children." She glanced over, realizing how little she knew about him. For all she knew he had a wife and a half-dozen kiddies stashed somewhere.

"Well, I don't," he said, apparently recognizing the question in her eyes. "What would you like to do now?"

She thought for a moment. "I still want to go to his cabin and see if I can get a glimpse of the fireplace inside." That had been her original plan.

"He may have just gone to the store."

"I'll be quick."

A few minutes later, Luc parked on the road twenty yards or so from the cabin. "I'll stand watch and alert you if he comes back."

"How?"

"I'll whistle."

Charlie was reminded of a line in an old Humphrey Bogart, Lauren Bacall movie she'd seen on late night TV. '*You remember how to whistle, don't you? You just put your lips together…and blow.*'

Smiling, Charlie got out and made her way to the cabin. It was twilight, but there was still enough light to see inside and it looked like Jean-Luc kept a few nightlights going. She skulked closer, reaching one of the windows near the back door at ground level. The cabin was on a small hill and she could see the front of it toward the lake had a deck where it would probably be easier to see inside.

Just as she neared the corner window and rose up on

her toes, she saw movement inside.

She ducked. Shit. Someone else was there. Jean-Luc's lover? No wonder he'd been angry. She'd interrupted his tryst? Okay, then. All she wanted was to see the damned fireplace. She took another step toward the corner near the deck in front. Maybe she could get a quick—

A door squeaked open. She jerked back. But if whoever it was went down to the lake...

She waited a moment, took one more step and peeked around the corner. A woman stood on the deck staring at the lake. A squeak of surprise caught in Charlie's throat. She shook her head. Jean-Luc's tryst was with a woman? She blinked. Watched the woman brush her long dark hair away from her face. Wait...a...minute. *No.*

Yes. It wasn't *just* a woman, it was Mia Powers. Even though her hair color was different, Charlie had looked at the woman's picture enough times to know it was Mia.

Her heart racing, Charlie flattened against the side of the cabin. Mia was alive and staying at her friend's cabin. She wasn't dead and buried by her former lover. But she was obviously hiding out.

Was she that afraid of the senator? Or was she a jilted lover getting even by stealing his files and letting him stew in his own hot water? Was she going to use the files for blackmail?

Too many questions.

When Mia turned and went back inside, Charlie hustled to the car, told Luc about Mia and regurgitated all the same thoughts she'd just had and ended with, "I think I need to talk to her."

"Someone was trying to kill us just two hours ago. I think it would be smart to go home and figure it out from a safe distance."

"If I don't talk to her now, she could leave and disappear again. And what if she knows what really happened to the senator's wife?"

"And if she does, then what?"

She blinked. "Justice. A woman is dead. The person responsible needs to pay for what he's done. Mia is the key. She must feel she's in danger, too, and if something happens to her—"

Luc touched her arm. "The senator is a powerful man. I do not want to see any harm come to you."

For a moment, she simply stared at him. What was he saying? Did he think the senator was behind the attempted hit? Was he in on what happened at the cabin and was trying to throw her off the trail she was following?

He took her hand, sincere concern in his eyes. Oh, man... "I-I appreciate that so much, Luc. But this is not about me. It's about a dead woman who needs someone to speak for her. To fight for her."

"But you are representing the senator."

She let out a long breath. "My father went to jail and was murdered because no one was there to speak for him. Too many innocents get hurt at the hands of the greedy and powerful, and that's exactly what's happening here. You're right. I can't do anything because the senator is my client. But if Mia knows something, she needs to come forward."

"You should be a prosecutor, not a defense attorney."

Charlie touched his cheek. Looked into his eyes. "You are thoughtful to be worried about me, but if it's within my power to somehow do something, I have to do it. If I can get Mia to come forward—"

She reached for the door handle. "I'm going to talk to Mia, try to convince her it's the right thing to do."

Silent, Luc nodded, even though she knew it was against his better judgement.

She kissed his cheek, opened the door and got out.

Watching her, Luc's chest nearly burst. Beautiful Charlize was a force to be reckoned with. A woman of passion and potential. She had no idea of her full potential, but he saw it coming alive before his very eyes. Unleashed, who knew what she was capable of...and he had to decide what to do with it. Before she ruined everything.

He'd spent a long time working out his plan to take out *El Diablo*. If Charlie exposed the senator, Luc's plan would fail. A mere cloud of suspicion over Mrs. Hawker's death, and the senator wouldn't be going on any hunting trips with the vice president.

He had to stop her. Had to think of some way to stall her. He needed another week.

But seeing the fires of justice burning in Charlie's eyes, he doubted he could do anything short of kidnapping her and keeping her locked in a room. In his business, innocent people sometimes got hurt. Charlie was one of the innocents—one who would get hurt because she was in someone's way. Unfortunately, in this case, his way.

If they had met many years ago…

He pushed away the thought.

They hadn't met back then. And he couldn't change history.

He was who he was.

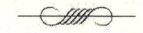

Charlie went directly to the door this time, rang the bell and knocked hard. When no one answered she knocked again. "Mia, I know you're there. I'm an attorney and I'm here to help you."

Nothing.

"Please, Mia. You can't hide out forever, and if I found you, you know the senator can find you, too. You are not safe here anymore. Please talk to me. I can help you."

A long moment later, the door creaked open and Mia Powers, the woman Charlie'd thought dead and buried in the woods, stood right there in front of her. Her hair was dark again, longer, and wearing a Detroit Tigers sweatshirt and faded jeans, she looked like the college photo Charlie had seen. Except for the hair color.

Mia stood with her shoulder braced against the door. "Who are you?"

"Charlie Street. I'm an attorney with Reston, Barrett and Brown."

Mia's face went aghast. "You're *his* attorney. I saw you on the news." She scrambled to push the door shut.

Charlie braced her shoulder against the door. "Wait. Yes, I'm the senator's attorney, but I believe I know why you're hiding. I know what happened to his wife, and I think you're afraid of him because you think he'll hurt you, too."

The woman's eyes darted beyond Charlie.

"He's not here. I'm alone. It's just me. Please let me come in and talk to you for a minute. I can help. I promise you I can help."

"Why should I believe you? How do I know you want to help? How do I know you're not going to go back to…him…with everything you know?"

Good questions. "Because if I wanted to do that, I'd be here with the senator…or the police."

Mia stiffened.

"Because I talked to your mother and she's desperate to hear if you're dead or alive."

Mia closed her eyes, opened them again. "In a minute. Wait just a minute." The door closed.

Charlie waited. What was she going to do? Get a weapon?

A few moments later, the door slowly opened. "Make this quick. I have things I have to do."

Yeah, like pack your bags and run away, again. "I understand. Thank you."

Mia led Charlie into a large room with a natural stone fireplace that looked years and years old. The air smelled of charred cedar and pine, and *yes*, the fireplace was the one in the photograph. Jean-Luc was being protective, helping his friend. She wanted to smile. Everyone needed a friend like that, even if Jean-Luc's over-the-top acting was what had made Charlie suspicious.

On one side of the room was a large dining room table with a vintage chandelier hanging low overhead, and on the other side, an L-shaped sectional centered in front of the fireplace. Old, worn furniture. Nothing fancy. Comfortable. "Mind if I sit?" Charlie asked, pointing to the couch.

Mia pulled out a dining room chair, scraping the dark oak flooring as she dragged the chair away from the table.

Oh-kay. Let's *not* get comfortable. Charlie smiled. "Thanks."

Mia sat in a wooden dining chair, too, placed her clasped hands in her lap. "What is it you think you can help me with?"

Mia's hands trembled in her lap and in that moment, Charlie realized she had no choice here…even though it would mean her job. She had to help this woman. "It's a long story, but let me say first…I promise to help you. Please believe me." She touched Mia's arm. Took a breath.

"You're right. The senator is my client, but in looking for the information to work on his case, I discovered a lot of other information…including the duffle bag you left in a locker at The Centerfold."

Mia's eyes lit. "You found it?" Her hands went to her mouth.

"Yes." Did she not remember where she'd left the bag?

"Ohmygosh. Do you have it? Was there anything in it?"

"No. I don't have it with me, but it's safe. Everything is safe, including the hard drive and necklace." She tilted her head to look at Mia. "Did you forget where you left it? I thought you might've left it in the locker on purpose."

"No, no. A friend took it for me when I didn't know what to do, and Jean-Luc said I could hide here. No one knew about this place, so I believed I'd be safe. But I didn't want it with me, and I didn't dare contact anyone after that. And since I trusted my friend…" Tears welled in her eyes.

"It's okay. Take your time," Charlie said, though anxious to hear more.

"I was going to give the information to the police, but then, when those men came to my place and tore it apart, I realized I was in danger. If they didn't find what they were looking for they would kill me. So, Jean-Luc brought me here and gave the duffle bag to Bunny. I didn't dare make contact with Bunny after that."

"And the senator? What was he doing during all this?"

"I don't know. I sent him a letter that said he had to leave me alone or I was going to give the information to the police."

"Didn't you think he could find you?"

"I took a plane to Mexico, then returned using my stepsister's passport with her married name on it. That's when I took…"

She stopped. Whatever she was going to say, she wasn't comfortable enough with Charlie to say it. Yet. "Well, I don't know all that's on the hard drive, but I some of it the senator doesn't want exposed. He as much as told me it's incriminating evidence. Maybe the stuff he's been accused of."

Mia nodded.

"And now that you will have it again, you can do what you set out to do in the first place."

If Mia took the information to the police, a warrant could be issued to search his properties and their premises. Hopefully the pill bottles would be found. It could all work out, and Charlie wouldn't be involved.

Mia shook her head. "I don't know if I can do that now."

"But you have to." Charlie rose to her feet. "His wife is dead. The same could happen to you. And the senator would get away with everything."

"I'll go away. Somewhere safe. Change my name. Start a new life."

"But why? Do you want to run and hide out for the rest of your life?" It didn't make sense. She had to convince the woman to do the right thing.

The just thing.

Charlie saw some photos on the mantel, one of Jean-Luc with another guy. The same as the one in his home. Some antique toys were on the floor. A basket of wood for the fireplace. "The photos you'd left in the bag, the one standing by the fireplace…that's what led me here."

"The photos?"

"One with you standing in front of a fireplace." She glanced over. And your mother mentioned Jean-Luc." She smiled, her gaze darting, taking in the layout, where the bedrooms might be located. "Everyone needs a good friend like Jean-Luc."

"Yes. I don't know what I would have done without him."

"There was also a diamond necklace in the bag."

Mia's expression soured. "Alvin gave it to me the very day his wife died. I was horrified. I never wore it. I wouldn't have even if I hadn't discovered what happened to her."

Charlie got up, walked to the corner near the fireplace and picked up a teddy bear. Held it up. "I've seen one of these before."

Mia's eyes went wide.

Just then she heard the front door open. A few seconds later, Luc came into the room. "What's going on?" He looked from Charlie to Mia and back again.

Mia's mouth flattened, eyes narrowing as she stepped away. "You lied! You said you were alone."

"I-I am. He just drove me up here, that's all. He doesn't have anything to do with this."

"And you're lying right now. I know who he is. I watch the news. He works for the senator. You brought him here to take me back, didn't you!" She turned and bolted toward the door leading to the lake.

Like a lightning strike, Luc reached out, curled his arm around Mia and drew her back.

"No, you're wrong," Charlie said quickly. "He does work for the senator, but he's helping me. He knows what happened, too. He brought me here, and he was with me when I found your bag..." She looked at Luc, but he wasn't looking at her. His gaze darted, his eyes had a strange hard look, one she'd never seen before. Sudden images of all the times he'd miraculously appeared on scene to help her clicked off in her head.

In that one single moment, an awful realization seeped through her. Her heart stalled. Trusting Luc might have been the biggest mistake of her life.

Her mouth dry, she cleared her throat. "Luc—" she

stated forcefully, "—is here to help. Aren't you, Luc!"

His expression pinched, as if he was thinking or listening to something else, then he snapped out of it. "Yes. Of course, Ms. Street."

CHAPTER TWENTY

"AUNTY MIA, CAN I come out now?" a small voice sounded from behind Charlie.

She swung around just as Mia ripped herself away from Luc and ran toward a little boy. Reaching him, Mia wrapped the child in her arms. "I have company here right now, sweetie, and we're talking about big people stuff. It won't be much longer." Her gaze went to Luc. "When these nice people go, we'll make some S'mores." She turned to the boy again and ruffled his hair. "Okay?"

"Here, Zack," Charlie said, handing the child the teddy bear. The same kind she'd seen in Senator Hawker's son's room at the senator's cabin."

"Oh, my Teddy." The child reached out, snatched the stuffed animal and hugged it.

Charlie looked at Luc, then back to the boy. "We'll only be a few minutes longer."

Whatever Luc had been thinking before seemed to switch off, and looking at the child, Luc's eyes warmed. He nodded. Then smiled.

Mia scooted the child off, and seeing him trundle off to his room, carrying his Teddy bear, Charlie could barely stitch two thoughts together. Oddly the only thought that did come together was that Mia must've gotten a duplicate bear for Zack so he would feel more comfortable away from home.

But what was the woman thinking. Kidnapping? No wonder she didn't want to go to the police.

Both Charlie and Luc turned to Mia.

"Why?" Charlie asked. "How?"

Mia glanced to the hallway, her voice quiet when she said, "He was being abused. I realized when I was in Mexico that I couldn't leave him in that environment. So, I planned my return when the senator was out of town for a few days with only a sitter at the house. I still had my key and, with Jean-Luc's help, I went to Zack's room at night and took him."

Mia glanced from Charlie to Luc, her eyes pleading. "The senator is a vicious and vengeful man when he's angry, and he gets that way a lot when he's drinking. Zack has already had one broken arm."

On her last words, her chin raised, as if she'd found some kind of resolve. "I won't go back. And I won't let you take him."

Charlie shook her head. "That's the last thing I want to do. But don't you see...now, if you let the police know what happened and show them you have the files to prove—"

"But I don't. You say you have the files, but you've given me no reason to believe you."

"I have the files and will gladly give them to you, but I can't help you get them to the police."

"Where are they then? Maybe you destroyed them already. How do I know I can trust you? You already lied to me twice."

Charlie went over to Luc, moved his arm and lifted his jacket, showing the blood on the front of his shirt.

Mia gasped.

"Some men tried to kill us when we were at the senator's cabin. Luc got rid of them, injuring one, but for all we know they are out there right now. And if they know Zack is here..."

"Ohh," Mia's breath caught, eyes widening. She shook her head, backed a step away.

Charlie took out her phone. Flipped to the photos she'd taken. "I took these on the boat. The medications are the kind that are difficult to detect in the body. I would love to see Mrs. Hawker's body exhumed to find out if the senator was responsible. But I was trespassing on the senator's boat when I took the photos, so I can't do that. If the hard drive has information that will get the authorities out to the house, they will find the same thing I did. But they need a reason for a search warrant."

Mia covered her face with her hands. "This is a nightmare. A total nightmare."

"If you and Zack come with us you'll be safer than you are here." She looked at Luc. "I can find a safe place for you to stay while we work out a plan. I'm not going to let anything happen to you or to Zack. I mean that."

Luc had been rooted to the same spot since Zack came out of the room, then finally, he took a step to stand next to Charlie when he spoke to Mia. "You were right to protect the boy. He needs your protection now more than ever. You are no longer safe here."

It was dark by the time they got on the road and because they didn't want Zack to hear anything bad and get scared, they spoke very little the entire time. Once Luc tuned in to some smooth jazz station, Zack slept most the way back to Detroit. The music also soothed Charlie's jittery nerves, allowing her thoughts to finally come together, and by the time they arrived at Charlie's mother's house, she had a plan. She just hoped she could convince Mia to go along with it.

Charlie had given her mother advance warning and told her not to ask questions and promised she'd explain when she could. She wasn't sure how in the world she'd explain without telling her what was actually going on, but it just didn't seem right for anyone to know until all was over and done with.

She didn't even tell Luc. Because at this point, it was better that no one knew what was on that hard drive. If Charlie didn't know, she couldn't be accused of breaching confidentiality.

She thanked Luc for helping, kissed him on the cheek, and told him she'd be in touch in the morning.

The minute Luc was gone and Mia went to get Zack comfortable in the extra bedroom, Charlie's mother motioned her daughter to follow her into the kitchen and then, standing with her arms crossed and legs apart, she glared at Charlie, her blue, blue eyes sparking fire. "Are we starting a safe house again?"

It wasn't exactly that, at least not in the same way as in the past when she'd needed a safe place for an abused spouse who refused to go to the usual non-profit places set up to house women and children in dangerous situations. But her mother didn't need to know the details. Like Luc, the less she knew, the better.

Except she had a feeling her mom wasn't going to let it go without a fight. Diana O'Meara Street's Irish temper was as fiery as her naturally curly red hair. She was nosey as hell when it came to what her kids were doing, and when she didn't get the information she wanted, that firebrand temper could flare to bonfire size in a nanosecond.

"It's not for long, Mom. I'll come by to get her tomorrow or the next day." Depending on when she could set their plan in motion.

Her mom went to the fridge and took out a bottle of some kind of wine and two glasses. Charlie motioned and shook her head, no. "Not for me, thanks. I've got work to do when I get home."

"The other glass isn't for you," Diana said and poured a glassful. "I have company coming over."

Charlie did a double-take. She glanced at the faux antique clock on the wall. "Now? It's late." She couldn't imagine any of her mother's few friends coming over at nine p.m.

"It's not late. Not really. Besides, my friend had to work late."

"Your friend?" She knew all of her mother's friends and raised her hands, palms up.

"No one you know. I was trying to tell you on the phone when you called earlier that it'll be difficult to have people here now that I'm dating."

Charlie almost spewed her spit. She'd encouraged her mom to think about dating, but she didn't really think she'd do it. Her mom had loved Charlie's dad so much that after he was murdered, the woman had gone into mourning for over twenty years.

"I think I'll have that wine now," Charlie said, walking over. She poured herself a glass and took a sip before asking, "Who is it? What do you know about him?" Her mouth puckered at the bad wine. "Ew. What is this stuff?"

"It's just someone who knows your uncle Emilio. We talked quite a bit today and finally tonight, right before you called, we decided to get together. And that's good wine. I got it as a gift when I retired."

Charlie took another sip, made another face. "You don't know this guy, but you invited him here tonight."

"It was difficult for him to get away sooner, and he's working in the area."

"Did Uncle Emilio set this up?" Somehow she doubted that. Her uncle had acted as their surrogate father ever since Charlie's dad died. He'd been protective of the whole family.

"Of course he did. How else would he get my number?"

"When did you first start talking with this guy?"

Her mom pursed her lips. She'd recently retired from her job as an art teacher and Charlie and Landon had worried she didn't have anything to keep her busy. But inviting strange men to her house without even meeting over a cup of coffee first wasn't what Charlie had in mind.

"How does he know Uncle Emilio? Why did he call?"

Diana's jaws clenched. "What difference does it make? We have a lot in common."

"It makes a difference because he could be a serial killer. Or someone who followed us, someone who wants to…" She glanced toward the hallway, lowered her voice. "…harm Mia and Zack."

Diana frowned, plopped down on a kitchen chair. "That doesn't make sense. I don't know how someone who knows your uncle would know anything about—" She waved a hand toward the hallway. "—them."

Charlie sighed. "Exactly. He wouldn't. But if someone wanted to gain your trust, telling you he knows Uncle Emilio would be a good way to do it."

Looking incredulous, Diana scoffed. "That's just silly. How would he get my name or your uncles?"

"Anyone can get anything online. Names, relationships. Nothing is secure anymore." Someone looking for Charlie would for sure check all her haunts. Her mom's. The gym. It had happened more than once before when she was a public defender.

She'd learned fresh out of law school that lawyers aren't the most popular people in the world. When she'd been threatened by both the Detroit mafia, and the Detroit police department, she knew it was time for a change. Since working for RB&B, all she'd come up against was the IRS and they had a different way of making threats.

Her mom swallowed the rest of her wine and poured another glass. "What should I do?"

Pacing, Charlie said, "Call him back and tell him something has come up. A family emergency. You're suddenly sick." She stopped, shrugged and threw her hands palms up. "I don't know, just call, tell him he can't come over, and see what he says."

Her mom left the room and seconds later came back with her cell phone.

"We need to get you a new phone."

"This one works fine." Diana opened the old flip-top phone and glanced at the screen. "Here it is." She called, and then stopped, her eyes rounding as she read something on the tiny screen. "That's strange. It's not in service." She glanced at Charlie. "I don't understand."

Charlie took out her own phone and punched in Luc's number. "Well, I do."

CHAPTER TWENTY-ONE

IT TOOK LUC less than five minutes to pull up in front of Charlie's mother's old Victorian house in Corktown. Given his history, Luc had probably been sitting outside someplace close so he could tail her again when she left.

As much as she needed his help, she still had a niggling feeling that something wasn't right. He worked for the senator who was paying him, and paying well it seemed. How could she truly trust him to look out for them? If the senator knew, Luc would lose his job for sure.

And if he couldn't be trusted, why save her from the thugs who'd broken into her condo intent on getting the hard-drive? If those men worked for the senator, too, maybe Luc had simply told them to leave and that he'd handle it?

Except he'd injured one of the men who'd shot at them at the senator's cabin. And he'd given her a gun. Or was that a way to get her to trust him. For all she knew, there were only blanks in the gun. But those men. And the blood.

That was real. Freaking real. And she wished she had Luc's gun right now.

The worst part was that she had no choice. She had to trust Luc. Trust that he'd do the right thing. She opened the door. "You didn't get very far, did you," she said, motioning him inside.

He glanced at her from under his brows. "This is true." He continued in to the living room and indicated the antique couch. "It looks very frail."

Nothing else. No explanation. She grinned. Damn him. "It's fine. Have a seat."

Charlie's mother was intent on keeping the interior of the historic home intact, right down to the quill-like ink pens on the period desk in the corner. The exterior had to meet certain codes since Corktown had been designated an historic district in the city. One of the few renovated areas.

"Sorry if I seem obtuse," Diana said. "But what are we doing? Why is he here again?" She gave Luc a long look, as if he were the one keeping her from her so-called date.

"He's a good friend and he can keep us safe." She hoped.

Luc stood, came over and bowed a little from the waist. "I am at your service, Mademoiselle." He flipped open one side of his leather jacket to reveal a holstered gun.

Diana gasped and took a step back.

"Do you have the other one handy," Charlie asked, glancing to his ankle.

A broad smile emerged as he looked at her. "Ah, Bonita, one lesson is not enough, especially when it is critical to actually hit something."

Heat rose from her chest up her neck to her face. "I didn't mean—"

A loud banging on the door made her jump. Shots rang out. *Pop, pop, pop.*

Luc moved so fast Charlie saw but a blur as he swooped both Charlie and her mother into the hallway and simultaneously pulled his gun. He reached down and pulled a gun from his ankle holster. "Here," he said and placed it in her hand. "You may need this."

Charlie stared at weapon in her hand. Her mother stood there, mouth agape.

"Go into the bedroom and lock the door." He urged her forward toward the bedroom door. "If necessary, just aim and pull the trigger like I showed you before."

In the next instant he was gone.

"What's going on?" Mia asked, peering out from the doorway to the guest room, Zak clinging to her leg.

"C'mon," Charlie said to her mom and hustled her into the bedroom with Mia and Zak. Still in the hall she said, "Lock the door after me and call the police."

Luc moved with catlike swiftness to the side of the tall, narrow window in the living room facing the street. About to pull the lace curtain aside and glance out, more gunshots rang out blasting through the front door. Within seconds the door splintered, as if rammed from the outside, and flew open.

Two men burst into the room, both wearing SWAT uniforms and equipment, AK47s raised.

Luc dropped his gun. "I'm unarmed," he shouted, but wasn't sure that mattered. Wasn't even sure they were real cops.

"Down on the ground," one said.

Luc obeyed. One man approached and kicked Luc's gun across the room to the side. From his position on his belly, Luc saw the guy's shoes. *Fuck! Not cops.* Just as the man reached him, Luc grabbed the guy's foot, pulled him off balance, and sprang to a low crouch and head butted him in the stomach, shoving him into the other fake cop. With a quick kick upward he clipped the second guys chin and he went sailing into the wall and slid down, out cold.

Ready to take out both men for good, a third guy appeared in the doorway, a pistol in his hand and aimed at Luc's chest. "Stop right there," he said. "Where is she?"

"Where is who?" Luc smiled, inched a hair closer. The guy was too far away and could shoot before Luc could reach him.

"The woman you were with"

Sirens wailed in the distance.

The fake cop shifted his feet. The two men on the floor stirred. "Hey, get up you idiots." He kicked one guy in the shin and the other in the ribs, but he kept his eyes on Luc.

The siren's sounded closer. "Get up!" he screamed. Both dudes dragged themselves to their feet and headed for the door.

The fake cop's eyes darted. He shifted from foot to foot, backing toward the door, too. "You've got to the count of three to tell me where she is or you're a dead man," he spat out.

"She's right here. And you've got no time," Charlie's voice came from Luc's right.

Just as he turned and saw her, gun raised, she shot. Twice. *Bam! Bam!*

The fake cop screamed as the gun flew from his hand and blood splattered all over Charlie's mother's Victorian sofa. Luc leaped forward to get his gun and as he did, the fake cop ran out the door. Luc burst out the door after the *pendejo*, but saw the man hurl himself into a dark sedan and speed away, a police car in pursuit.

Luc holstered his weapon, turned and went back inside.

"Sorry," Charlie said, rushing up next to him. "I couldn't lock myself in and leave you out here alone."

He raised a brow. "You do not trust my abilities?"

She grinned. "I do. But everyone needs a little help now and then."

"And good help it was. I think you weren't telling me the truth when you said you didn't know anything about guns."

"No. I mean, yes, it's true, I don't know anything. But he was going to shoot you, so I did what you told me before. Aim and shoot."

He swallowed, not wanting to think of how many ways that could have gone wrong.

"I had to do something, or at least try."

He'd never had help from anyone in his life, and he'd learned a long time ago that those who did help usually wanted something in return.

But not Charlize Street. She had no reason to help him. Other than that's who she was. She'd saved his life.

And she'd probably regret it in the end.

CHAPTER TWENTY-TWO

CHARLIE HANDED THE GUN to Luc, her hands still shaking. "The police can't know about Mia and Zak being here."

"I know." Luc sat with her on the couch as she texted her mom in the bedroom. *Everything's okay, but the police will be here soon about the break-in. We don't want them to see Mia, so take a flashlight and go to the attic with Mia and Zak. Stay there until I text you to come down.*

In the bedroom closet, there was a dropdown stairway to the attic, a quiet place where Charlie used to go as a kid when she wanted no one to bother her.

"I'm going to leave," Luc said. "Otherwise we'll have a lot of explaining to do and the senator will know everything. Tell the police it was a home invasion and one of the idiots fired a shot and hit the other one."

She nodded as he turned and headed for the back door. She wasn't about to tell the Detroit P.D. anything other than what Luc said. The city government had been so corrupt and on the take when Kwame Kilpatrick was in office, she didn't know who she could trust not to tell the senator about Mia and Zak.

Besides, they were so busy looking for arsonists who were setting fires around Detroit a dozen times a day, it took forever for the police to respond to a minor burglary. It was going to be up to Mia to tell them once they had a fail-safe plan...and Charlie still wasn't sure how all that was going to go down.

It was another thirty minutes before the police arrived, and when they did, they didn't seem particularly interested in the home invasion. After all, it happened in Corktown, not Grosse Pointe, where all the politicians lived. The P.D. would've been on that in a flash.

One of the officers bagged a pillow that had blood on it and told her they'd have it analyzed and see if they could get a match and within twenty minutes, they were gone.

Charlie sighed. If they did get a match, it was unlikely the fake cops were going to tell anyone why they'd been there.

And if they did, it would be long after her plan was carried out.

Charlie got up and went to the attic. "It's okay to come down now." She pulled down the rope to the stairs.

Diana came down first, eyes wide and her curly red hair looking like a clown wig. "It's okay," Charlie said to Mia who came down next. "No one knows you're here."

Mia took a deep breath, obviously relieved. Charlie looked at Zack. "You okay, sweetie?"

He nodded, still clutching his stuffed Teddy bear. "But you found us, so we lose, don't we?"

Frowning, Charlie looked at Mia.

"Hide and seek is like that," Mia said to the boy. "But we're good sports. We'll play another game another time, but right now, I think it's time for you to hit the sack. Can you say good night to everyone?"

"Night," Zack said, as Mia directed him down the hall toward the bedroom again. "I'll be back," Mia whispered over her shoulder and then followed Zack.

"What the hell was that all about?" Diana spat out when Mia was gone.

"We don't know," she lied. Mia had to know, but the less her mother knew, the better. "The police were chasing some guys who'd robbed a store. They thought that's who they were." And given the crappy neighborhoods nearby, it could easily happen.

"I thought it might be Mia's husband." Diana glanced at Mia, just returning. "Or whoever you're running away from."

"It doesn't matter," Charlie said. The police will find the creeps and take care of it. And Mia and Zak will be gone in a couple of days."

"I'm really sorry to impose on you like this," Mia said to Diana.

"Oh, my dear." Diana rushed to Mia's side and gave her a hug. "It's not an imposition. I'm happy to help." She crossed to the breakfront cabinet, her gaze narrowed at Charlie. "It was a surprise, that's all, and I didn't have time to prepare."

"The problem," Charlie said, "is that there's rarely time since it's usually an emergency situation." Then under her breath to her mom, "Hard for some people to understand."

Diana raised her chin. "Nevertheless, you are welcome here, Mia. You and your son." She turned and smiled at both of them. "I don't know about anyone else, but I need a glass of wine."

Laughing, Charlie said. "Sure, Mom. I think we could all use one right now."

CHAPTER TWENTY-THREE

WARM SEPIA LIGHT from a streetlamp outside Charlie's mom's house shone on the deserted street, like a scene from an old black and white noir movie.

The police had been there and gone. No one knew Mia and Zack were at her mom's house. If Charlie stayed, she might be putting everyone in danger. She decided her apartment would be okay since the thugs had already been there and not found anything. Except when they'd shouted that they wanted her.

Maybe they thought they could torture her for the information. A chill ran up her spine at the thought. Her dilemma was answered when Luc texted that he'd be there to pick her up. She didn't know what he had in mind, but it didn't matter. He would protect her. That's all she needed to know.

"I feel so stupid," Diana said, coming into the living room where Charlie was watching for Luc.

Charlie turned as her mom came up beside her. She reached out, wrapped an arm around her mom and pulled her close. They'd had so many clashes that someone else looking in might think they hated each other. The truth was exactly the opposite. Charlie was too much like her mother that was all, both willing to die for a cause they believed in. But as much as they were alike, they were total opposites.

Diana's shiny outlook had never been tarnished by the reality of the world they lived in. Diana believed things would always get better. The sun would always shine. Bad things happened, but there was always more good than bad in the world.

Charlie wasn't convinced. Not since she was eight years old. Things could get better, but they never stayed that way. The sun might shine, but tornadoes, hurricanes, blizzards and bad people could tear things apart. Things might improve after bad things happened, but it was always temporary...until the next earthquake or mass murder. Charlie didn't believe she was as cynical as her mother often accused, but she was realistic.

"There's no way you could've known, Mom."

Her mom smiled up at her. "Maybe not. But I was being stupid thinking I could ever find anyone who could take your father's place."

"No one could do that, but that's not the point of dating."

"No? Then what is?"

"I think the idea is to find someone who compliments your life in a way no one else can."

Car lights flickered outside.

"I have to go, Mom. Text me, keep me posted on Mia and Zak. If anything at all happens, contact me immediately. I'll let you know when I'll be back to get them." Hopefully that would be as soon as possible. The longer things dragged out, the greater the chance of something going wrong.

"I sure wish I knew what's going on."

Charlie smiled, gave her mom a squeeze and went outside to meet Luc. She wished she did, too.

Luc, behind the driver's wheel of a big black Chrysler and wearing a Tigers baseball cap, a hoodie, and dark horn-rimmed glasses, motioned her inside. Once she settled, he reached behind the passenger seat and pulled out three bags filled with what looked like clothes. "It's the best I could do on short notice." I can get some of your own things later if you need them."

He pulled out, turned on the very next street, eyes on the rearview mirror half the time.

"It's only going to be a couple of days until I get things worked out," Charlie said.

"Good. You will be safe until then."

"Great. And the car?"

"It's a rental. Just taking precautions."

"Ah." Made sense. If someone was looking for them, they'd be looking for either her car or his Lexus. Probably the same reason for the baseball cap and casual clothes. He looked like a regular guy. She'd only seen him in expensive suits and fine leather. "I like the glasses."

He looked over, then back to the road. "Look in the bag."

She reached inside. "What the...?" She pulled out a blond wig.

"Put it on."

"Now?

"Now. The jacket, too. I don't want anyone to recognize you when we go inside."

She pulled down the visor, opened the mirror and smoothed her ponytail into a tight bun on the top of her head, then slipped on the long straight wig with bangs that swept to the side. Turning from side to side, she said, "Not bad."

Luc glanced over. Grinned. "Very nice. Now the rest."

Next she replaced the jacket and scarf she'd been

wearing with a black leather motorcycle type short jacket. Her camel colored sweater was only visible at the neck and a couple inches at the bottom.

"Shoes, too."

She pulled out a pair of sleek black ankle boots and replaced the tan leather she was wearing. It worked fine with her skinny black pants. "I think I need a motorcycle. You pick all this out?"

"I got it from a friend."

A revelation that brought all kinds of questions to mind.

"There are other necessities in there as well."

"I'm grateful, Luc. Truly. If it weren't for you, I don't know what I'd be doing right now."

Five minutes later, he pulled into the drive for the underground parking garage at the Renaissance City Club Apartments, punched in a code and drove inside.

"And we're here because?" She turned to him as he parked in a space next to the elevator. "Is this where you live?"

"No, the apartment belongs to a friend who's out of town for a few weeks. You will be safe here."

A lot safer than at her own place for sure. The Renaissance Club Apartments were so close to the offices of RB&B, she walked by all the time. They had security at all entrances. Whoever Luc's friend was, he had money. The apartments, she knew sold for up to two million. Maybe more.

At the elevator, Luc pushed the button for the top floor. The penthouse. Yes, Luc's friend definitely had money.

No one got off or on the elevator as they zipped to the top, and as far as she could tell, no one except the person manning the security cameras saw them. When they stopped, Luc went to the door, used some kind of code to get inside, tipped his head and swept an arm, motioning her to go before him. Low lights went on automatically as she entered. Luc came up beside her, took her hand and walked to the floor to ceiling windows in the open concept living area.

Her breath caught. "Oh, wow." The Detroit city skyline lay in silhouette before her, the Renaissance Center, the Fisher Building downtown, the vague outlines of the people mover, the Detroit River and the lights of Windsor twinkling on the other side.

"It is lovely, yes?" Luc said, smiling as he looked at her.

"It's incredible." She swung around. The apartment was nearly as gorgeous as the view.

"You are incredible," Luc said, reaching to touch her cheek. "Beautiful and incredible. I wish I could stay, but I have a call from the senator. Regretfully, I must go."

She regretted it, too, but she also had work to do. Keeping Mia and Zack safe was first and foremost in her mind. She'd been mulling over a plan, but it required Mia's help and she didn't know if the woman was up for it.

Charlie locked the door after Luc left, and then went to find the bathroom…a luxurious room of marble, shiny chrome and glass. A woman's silk robe and two thick velvety towels hung on hooks behind a soaker tub. A table on the other side held candles, fresh flowers, and a bottle of wine.

Yes, she regretted Luc had to leave. A lot.

She went into the adjoining bedroom, sat on the bed and pulled off her boots. She took off the wig, set it on the white down comforter, pulled the band from the bun and ran her fingers through her hair. As she looked around, she saw feminine touches, the flowery paintings, vases of flowers, a throw placed in the perfect position on an overstuffed chair. No, it didn't feel like a guy's apartment. Not at all.

She got up and went to the wall of mirrored closet doors. Pushed open one side.

The closet was the size of her condo living room, and was filled with clothes and a wall of shoes. Women's shoes. She crossed to a dresser with shelves above it holding several hats and wigs. And a photo of a beautiful blond woman wearing fatigues and carrying what looked like an assault weapon.

Her stomach clenched. Luc had an interesting friend.

"As you know, Luc, I reward loyalty from my employees. I expect a lot and I reward those who show me they can do what needs to be done. Are you one of those guys, Luc?"

The last guy who wanted Luc to pledge his loyalty belonged to the Mexican Cosa Nostra. And he was no longer among the living. The senator had been working with the Detroit mafia, the Partnership, so perhaps what needed to be done was something the senator had to do for them? The stupid man had no idea how the Partnership would use narcissistic power hungry egomaniacs like the senator for their purposes, then dump them into a barrel of lye when they were done with them.

Not a bad thing if it saved Luc the trouble. He just needed the senator to go on his hunting trip with the vice president before that happened. Then Luc would be gone. His one regret was that he would miss his beautiful Charlize, the first woman who'd made him wish he wasn't who he was.

"I am, Senator. You have witnessed this, have you not?"

"I have. You have done your job well. I need that kind of person in my employ. I need someone who will not disappoint me. No matter what the job is."

"I am at your service, Senator."

"Good. Very good. And if I need someone to be gone from my life, you can take care of that little business for me, can you?"

The hair on the back of Luc's neck prickled. Take care of that *little business*. A hit. When the government asked, there was a good reason. Sticking around to take out the V.P. was good reason. He'd been waiting for years to make it happen. "I can, senator. I'm very good at taking care of business for my employers." Especially if it kept him around long enough to do what he came here to do.

"Good. Come by tomorrow morning and we'll talk more. It should be easy since you've already been working with the person I need gone."

CHAPTER TWENTY-FOUR

CHARLIE SAT AT her desk at Reston, Barrett and Brown, nerves snapping under her skin as she waited for her meeting with the senator. Her mouth and throat were so dry, she wasn't sure she could produce a single word. She chugged half a bottle of water, swishing the last swallow around in her mouth. Her heart raced, blood pounded in her ears. Soon.

It would all be over soon.

She picked up the hard drive on her desk. Her lips tipped up in a wry smile. Who had who by the short hairs now?

Loud voices came from outside her office and, seconds later, the senator banged open her door, charged inside and stopped when his thighs hit her desk. Luc was directly behind and closed the door.

"Senator Hawker." Charlie nodded and smiled. "I'm glad you could make it."

"I'm not used to being summoned and expected to be somewhere on a moment's notice, Ms. Street. And to be honest, I've been having some serious second thoughts about letting Douglas talk me into having you represent me."

"Please sit, Senator. I have good news for you."

He scowled, hands palms up, as if he didn't know how she could possibly have good news. He turned to look at Luc, nodded, and then sat in the client chair. "About damned time I had some good news."

"Would you like some water or coffee, Senator? I can have January bring some in if you'd like."

"I'd like to hear whatever it is you have to say, so I can get back to my golf game. Let's cut the bullshit and get on with it."

She took a breath and cracked open another bottle of water she'd stashed under her desk. "Yes. Okay. No more bullshit."

The senator pulled back "What?"

"I said no more bullshit. I just wanted to tell you that everything is going to work out perfectly. We found your records and once we look at them we can verify there was no...uhm... misuse of state funds to hire prostitutes from the—"she held up a notepad, squinted to read "—Devonshire Escort Service, and to use state monies to throw lavish champagne parties for your cronies." She ran her finger down the pad. "Oh, yes, and there's the thing about funneling questionable funds into offshore bank accounts." She tilted her chin, raised her hands and smiled. "See. No more bullshit."

"What? What the hell did you just say?" The senator's face reddened. He glanced to Luc, who looked a little surprised himself. Eyes wide, Luc shrugged.

"Is this some kind of joke or-or..." the senator sputtered, words apparently not coming as swiftly as when he was on the campaign trail. "This is an outrage. There's no way you have that information."

Charlie lifted the hard drive on her desk with two fingers. "Really?"

One side of the senator's mouth curved in a sneer. He leaned forward. "What are you trying to prove, Ms. Street?"

"I'm trying to prove exactly what you wanted me to,

senator. And the information on this hard drive is the proof the court needs. That should make you feel one-hundred percent better."

The senator laughed, his voice raising an octave. "I don't know where you got that, but if that's the hard drive that bitch stole from me, it belongs to me, Ms. Street. I don't know what you're trying to pull here. You're my attorney. Anything you've obtained in the course of this investigation is confidential, so you can't give it to anyone."

Standing, Charlie sighed. "Yes. You're absolutely right about the confidentiality, Senator. But I didn't say I was giving the records to anyone. Someone else has already done that. The information was subpoenaed a long time ago and I understand it is in the hands of the Attorney General's Office as we speak." She smiled again.

Mia Powers entered the room and walked to Charlie's side. "Hello, Alvin."

Hawker snapped out a hand, grabbed the hard drive, threw it on the floor and stomped on it until the plastic was in small fragments, his face crimson, veins popping out on his neck like a bas relief map.

Mia came around to look at the crushed hard drive, put a hand to her mouth. "Oh, shoot. You just ruined my knitting patterns."

Charlie came around and stood next to Mia. "As I said, Senator, I don't have any choice. The court requested the records, so Mia had to turn them over to the Attorney General's Office."

"There were also a few other things in your files that were pretty interesting, Alvin," Mia said. "I think the grand jury will be looking at all that, too."

The senator's face knotted. His eyes shone like the devil incarnate. And in one quick step he grabbed Mia's arm, yanked her to his chest and pulled a gun. "You bitch." He held the gun at Mia's head, then, as if he couldn't decide what to do, aimed it at Charlie. "You did this. She's too dumb to do any of it." He raised his grip to curl his arm around Mia's neck, but held his gun on Charlie.

Charlie's heart banged in her chest. She knew what it felt like to shoot a gun and she knew what it was like to get shot at. She wasn't about to find out what it was like to eat a bullet. "Senator. Please put the gun down. You're just going to make things worse."

He laughed. His gaze darted, eyes searching, door to windows. "Make things worse?" He spat out. "I don't know if that's possible. And if I'm going down it isn't going to be because of you two cunts." He waggled the gun at Charlie. "I'm going to leave here and I'm taking you along. Get over here."

Charlie looked to Luc, standing like a statue near the door. She couldn't see his eyes behind the dark glasses. Why wasn't he doing anything? He had expert skills. He could kill people, he'd said.

But he didn't move.

Blood pounded in her ears. He worked for the senator. Had he simply been keeping track of her until she led him to the hard drive? Her chest tightened. *Oh, God.*

As Luc stood there stone-faced, she remembered his words. *Self-defense requires focus. No emotion.* She pulled a lungful of air. Narrowed her eyes on the senator. Sucked more air to steady her voice. "Please, Senator. Think about your legacy. You've done so much good for the state. People will remember that. But if you continue this now, that's all they will remember."

The senator grimaced at Charlie, a crazed sheen in his eyes. "Legacy? Are you kidding me?" His mouth turned up in a twisted sneer. "Do you think give a damn about any fucking legacy? Do you think the guys who really run this state care about that kind of shit? It's about money and power, and I have that in spades.

Enough to take you two bitches out without anyone blinking an eye."

He lunged at Charlie, his gun point blank at her forehead, Mia still sputtering in his chokehold grip like a rag doll. "Luc," Hawker shouted. "I need a little help here, bodyguard. What the hell are you standing there for? Get over here and take care of these bitches."

Luc didn't move. "That's not what I was hired for, Senator."

"Oh, I see. Greedy bastard are you?" The senator laughed. "Can't say I blame you. I'd do the same. Squeeze the bastards for more money when you can. Okay, then. You already agreed to it yesterday, so what's the going rate for a hit today? One hundred K? Two-hundred?"

Luc crossed to the senator, gave both women a cursory glance, placed his hand on his chin as he looked them over. He nodded. "Two women. Two Hundred."

The senator's mouth pinched.

"That's a good deal, Senator. These *bellas damas* are worth much more." Luc's eyes traveled from the tip of Charlie's head to her toes, then settled on her mouth.

Charlie's heart dropped like a stone. Mia's eyes bugged out as she struggled under the senator's grip. He jammed the gun into her temple, again. Mia froze. Charlie did, too. If she moved to grab the gun, it could go off in the scuffle. He could shoot both her and Mia.

If Luc didn't do it first.

Luc looked at the senator again, chin tilting as if to tell him to make up his mind.

"Okay. Okay. You drive a hard bargain, my man. Two-hundred then. You got it."

Luc held out his hand, a cold, hard smile on his face.

A chill ran up her spine. *Oh, God.* What now? She glanced back and forth between the two men and Mia, then the near surroundings. Her desk. What...what could she do? What...she eyed the letter opener, an outdated gift she'd never used.

The senator placed the gun in Luc's hand. Unnecessarily so since Luc had weapons of his own.

Charlie stiffened. *Fight or flight. Don't just freaking stand here.*

"C'mon," the senator barked, then shoved Mia toward Luc. Almost in the same motion, he yanked Charlie to him. "Take care of that one. I can have a plane to Venezuela waiting in twenty minutes. Do it, and let's get out the fuck out of here."

Luc motioned Mia to the other chair with his gun, keeping an eye on both women. "Are you sure, Senator?" Luc said. "The noise will draw attention."

"Okay. Then do it another way. A quiet way." He waved at Mia. "Her now. We'll take the attorney along until we know we're safely in Venezuela." He tightened his grip on Charlie's arm and curved his other arm around her groping her breasts. "On the way, I'm going to teach her a lesson she won't ever forget."

"*Un momento*, Senator," Luc said. "Take your hands off the *senorita*."

"Huh?" the senator said.

"You heard me." With record speed Luc was next to the senator, shoved the gun up the man's nostrils and with that, the senator's hold on Charlie loosened and she broke away. She flew to the desk, grabbed the opener and turned.

Luc had a pinch hold on the senator's neck, a move Charlie knew from her self-defense class, but couldn't remember what it was called. It could incapacitate a man, she remembered. The senator's dropped like a limp rag, but wasn't out, just stunned. And she had to decide if she was going to use the opener on anyone. Luc if necessary.

Hawker shook his head. "What the hell is wrong with you," he croaked out. "Shoot her."

Charlie tightened her grip on the opener. She couldn't move fast enough to get to either of them...and...and what the hell was Luc doing?

Luc crossed his arms, the gun still in one hand. "When I was a little boy," he said looking down on the senator. "I knew a man who was very cruel. He had no respect for women, either. One of those women was my mother, and I always said that someday I would make him pay for what he did. And I will. But right now, my plans have been compromised, and I have another job to do, thanks to you, Senator."

Luc spoke slow, his voice smooth and even. His tone, deadly quiet. Charlie heard the contained fury, saw his muscles vibrate. What the hell was going on? She could make a break for it and hope Luc wouldn't shoot her...or Mia. But the door was across the room. She'd never make it out of the path of a bullet. She'd just have to hope Luc wouldn't shoot.

The senator struggled to his feet. "What the fuck are you talking about?" He clutched at Charlie again and shoved her in front of him. "Let's move." She wanted to turn around and stab him in his fish mouth, instead, she dropped down and slammed a foot into his testicles.

The man crumbled, moaning and letting out a string of curses. Quickly she got behind him, got him in a one-arm choke hold and jammed the letter opener to his neck. She had no idea what Luc was going to do.

And he had the gun.

"Do it, Luc," the senator croaked. "Kill this bitch."

"No, Senator. That's not going to happen."

Luc looked at Charlie. "I think it is time for you to leave the room, *bonita*." He looked at Mia. "You go, too. And in about five minutes, you can call the police. The senator and I have something to discuss before they arrive."

Charlie wasn't about to stop and ask questions and

pushed Mia ahead of her out the door. Five minutes, Luc had said. What on earth for? He wasn't going to help Hawker get away was he? She needed to call the police now.

"What's going on," January quizzed, eyes rounding.

"There's a crazy man in my office. In five minutes we call the police."

"Why wait?" January reached for the phone but stopped short, waiting for Charlie's okay.

Luc had let them go…and she'd heard the fury in his tone when he mentioned his mother. God, she hoped he wasn't going to hurt the senator. But could she trust him to do the right thing? Hell, she didn't even know what that was at this point. Except that there were courts to take care of the senator.

Justice. When it worked right, there was nothing like it.

"Because Luc said so," Charlie said.

Mia looked at her as if she were crazy.

"It's okay, Mia," Charlie said almost to herself. "I trust him" And scary as this was, she realized she did trust him She hadn't known him long, but where she was concerned, she trusted Luc to do the right thing.

Waiting together at the January's desk, they all listened. Nothing. Not a sound. Finally Mia said, "I don't know what's going on with you and the bodyguard, but I like him." She turned to Charlie. "But I'm getting the feeling you like him, too." She smiled. "If you know what I mean."

Charlie knew. And she remembered what Luc had said the night they'd made love. He wasn't the man for her. As much as he wished he could be, he wasn't. "Yes. I know what you mean, Mia. I like him, too."

And as much as she might want things to be different, it could never be. She had no idea what secret life Luc led, and she was pretty sure now that she didn't want to know.

"Can I call the police now?" January had her phone in hand.

"Yes. It's time."

CHAPTER TWENTY-FIVE

"I'M FINE, MOM. I'm going to bed now." When Charlie hung up, she flipped on the news. Ever since they'd stayed at her mother's two weeks ago, her mom had been calling three times a day to make sure Charlie was okay.

The senator had been arrested for several crimes against the people of the state of Michigan, and there was a court order to exhume the senator's late wife's body. Charlie'd learned it was the senator who'd sent the men to retrieve the hard drive and broke her car window, and he'd also sent the two who'd attempted to kill her and Luc both times. But, according to the senator, he had not hired the men Luc had seen at the casino. She didn't know who they were or if they'd ever find out...unless they showed up again.

Mia was finally able to come out of hiding, Zack was with his grandparents, and although Mia would have to face some charges for kidnapping, the grandparents had assured her she could visit Zack if it was okay with the court. Mia had a good attorney, so Charlie knew the young woman would be offered some type of plea bargain and probably not do any time.

They'd called the police as directed, and when the SWAT team arrived at the law firm and went inside Charlie's office, they'd found the senator trussed with flexi-cuffs and handcuffed to a desk leg, his socks rolled up and stuffed in his mouth. And Luc was nowhere to be seen.

Since then, the only thing she'd heard about Luc was that the senator was screaming to be housed in a private cell, away from other prisoners. Apparently, Luc had warned the senator he would be meeting a few people in jail that Luc knew very well, and they had an intense dislike for people who abused children.

Luc was a mysterious man, one she'd realized had many demons to fight. She did, too, and, someday, maybe they would meet again under other circumstances. Who knew?

Right now, she was fending off reporters who were making her out to be some kind of super investigator, having uncovered both a murder and then rescuing a child who'd been kidnapped nearly a year earlier. No one, not the best investigators, or the police, had been able to find Zackary Hawker.

It was quite the accomplishment, she had to admit, and she'd already set up a couple of interviews with news stations. One newscaster was reporting about her as she sat there watching, but he made it even more sensational by adding, "Charlie Street is the daughter of convicted murderer, Alejandro Montoya Street, who died in prison twenty-two years ago at the hands of another inmate. The young attorney has been trying to prove her father's innocence ever since she went to law school. If she can do what she did in the rescue of Zackary Hawker, who was kidnapped over a year ago, and in uncovering the alleged murder of Penelope Hawker, Senator Alvin Hawker's late wife, we have no doubt she will succeed."

Charlie laughed and flipped the channel where another reporter said, "Two men were found murdered last night. Their necks had been broken, but there were no signs of other injuries or of theft. Police believe the men are the thieves who have been robbing casino patrons after watching them win large sums of money. It has been speculated that the mysterious deaths may be related to the robberies."

A photo of the two men, both with long records and a history of horrific violence, flashed on the screen. *Ohmygod.* The two men who'd robbed her. And robbed others, apparently. A quick moment of hope skittered through Charlie that maybe they'd recovered her money. But that fragile hope was dashed in the announcer's next sentence.

She clicked off the television. She would need money since she'd been asked politely to resign from her position at Reston, Barrett and Brown. Douglas had apologized profusely, especially since she'd brought more positive publicity to the firm than they'd had in years.

Because Mia was the one to bring the information to the police, Charlie hadn't technically breached confidentiality, but the partners decided she wasn't a 'good fit,' anymore. What they really meant was that she wasn't a puppet willing to do whatever was required of her by the firm. She didn't play by the rules, Douglas had said, and he had no choice but to ask her to resign. He'd said he was sure she'd be fine since all the publicity would bring customers to her door.

He might be right if she had the money to open the door. She couldn't just slap a sign on her condo and say open for business. There were costs involved in starting her own legal service, and, at the moment, she couldn't even pay her mortgage.

Two weeks later, she saw on the internet that the old hotel she wanted to purchase was going up for auction. She'd asked her bank for a loan, but without a job, it was a no. She'd tried to get an equity loan on her condo, but her credit wasn't good enough. Everywhere she turned, it was a no. So much for all the publicity she'd garnered.

So much for the theory about visualizing your dreams. She'd visualized until she was practically catatonic.

She settled down on the couch with a good Ann Voss Peterson thriller novel in hand. She'd forget all of it for a few hours at least. She'd barely read the first line when a loud knock at the door made her jump. Shit. Not another reporter. She was so tired of taking credit for something that had only happened in the course of investigating something else, that she wanted to scream.

In the wake of all the publicity she felt more like a fraud than ever, but the insatiable media kept stoking the fire. She went to the door and spoke without opening. "If you're a reporter, go away."

"It's FedEx delivery." She looked into the peephole. Saw a man wearing a uniform. When she opened the door, he shoved a sheet of paper toward her. "I need you to sign for the package, ma'am."

Ma'am. That was the second time someone had called her that. Or was it the third? If she was the maternal kind she might start worrying about her biological clock. She signed the slip and took the package. Closing the door, she noticed a small envelope was taped on top. She tore it off, no idea who might be sending her something.

A few weird things had happened since the senator was arrested. Like the creepy old man, who'd sent her flowers and asked if she'd marry him. And the woman, who'd set up a twitter fan page for Charlie...her hero. And someone who'd sent her a tiny Wonder Woman action figure. She liked that one and kept it on her desk for inspiration.

All well and good, but she knew how quickly it would all fade. Only the bad stuff sticks. And even with all the publicity, she was the same person in the same position she'd been in not that long ago.

No job and no money.

She went to the window and glanced out. Saw the FedEx guy get in his truck.

She opened the small envelope first. All it contained was a card with the name, Gabriel Weatherly, and an email address. Gabe…the man Luc had said could give her self-defense and gun training. An attorney.

And inside the box—twenty-five thousand, four hundred and forty-four dollars.

Please turn the page to read an excerpt from DETROIT RULES, book 2 in the Street Law series.

DETROIT RULES

Street Law: Whatever it takes…

Disillusioned attorney-turned private investigator Charlie Street's life shattered when her father was convicted of murder and killed in prison. Convinced he was framed, she's vowed to find who's responsible and see them pay.

Detective Remington Malone's best friend has disappeared…and not even the threat of losing his job can keep Remy from investigating. But as the bodies of his snitches start piling up, it's clear someone besides the chief of police wants to stop him.

Remy needs the best PI in town and that's Charlie Street. Except there's bad blood between Charlie and Detroit's finest—ever since they tricked her into telling where to find her father. The last thing Charlie wants is to work with a cop. But when she sees a link between Remy's case and her father's…it's a job she can't refuse. Soon, Charlie and Remy are mired in the dark world of human trafficking, running from the mob—and fixed in the crosshairs of a killer.

And…not everyone plays by the rules.

A ticked off mob boss, cops on the take, and a twisty road to redemption… *DETROIT RULES* is the second book in Linda Style's explosive STREET LAW series. Seduction, betrayal, and murder—it will take a lot more than money to fix this Motor City problem.

CHAPTER ONE

Three years later

GUILTY AS HELL.

And yet, an aura of doubt filled the room.

He studied the attorney, watched her draw each hand-picked jury member into her web.

The woman inhabited her role as if she were Meryl Streep giving another Oscar-worthy performance …every move skillfully choreographed.

The filled-to-capacity courtroom hummed with expectation as the attorney for the defense, Charlize Street, paused near the witness stand, adjusted her red curve-hugging suit jacket, and then took a step back, letting her audience wait just the right amount of time between each perfectly crafted sentence. Each word crisp and clear, every sentence succinct.

She wore a slim, black skirt, ending at the knee, allowing a glimpse of well-toned legs. The deep slit in the back drew his gaze upward to her best asset. Her shoes, while not five-inch stilettos, were definitely tall enough to make any juror with an ounce of testosterone take notice.

And like one of Pavlov's dogs, Remy's hormones responded on cue.

Never mind that she was defending the most

notorious madam in Detroit for a gruesome murder that would make Jack the Ripper's carnage seem like a kiddies' birthday party in comparison.

Yet, from the rapt expressions on the jurors' faces, Ms. Street had them right where she wanted. His brother was right. The woman was good. *Very good*.

Exactly the person he needed.

All he had to do was convince her she wanted him. And *that*, he'd heard, was about as likely as drowning in the desert.

He tugged the neck of his shirt. The acrid scent of too many people in a too-hot room permeated the air like foul exhaust fumes during a Motor City rush hour. Even so, the attorney for the defense stayed cool...in total control.

The defendant shifted in her chair, her gaze cast down, her attitude far different than when Remy had arrested her sixteen years ago working hooker central on Eight Mile.

Madam Lucy Devonshire now hired top-dollar models to do the work for her, but she was still a prostitute. And a murderer.

And she was going to walk.

Thanks to her hot-shot lawyer, Charlize, AKA Charlie, Street, the defendant would be back pimping her girls to horny millionaires within minutes of the verdict.

Cops got the sleaze off the streets and slick attorneys got them off the hook.

But then...what was one more killer on the streets of *Murder City*. Getting rid of one baddie was like swatting mosquitoes in the Okefenokee Swamp.

Remy clenched his jaw. Swallowing his dislike for attorneys was nothing compared to what he was willing to do to find out what happened to Adam.

Nothing compared to what he'd do if he found the

son of a bitch responsible for his best friend's disappearance.

In the back of the room sitting next to Hank Hitchens, a retired detective with the Detroit PD whom Remy hadn't seen in years, Remy drew in a lungful of air. Rolled his shoulders. Focused on his goal—Charlie Street, attorney extraordinaire, defender of the poor…and street slime who thought the law didn't apply to them.

"You involved?" Hitchens whispered and tipped his head toward the bench.

"Nope," Remy mouthed and shook his head.

The older man leaned closer to Remy. "This one's gonna take down a lotta good people."

They always did. When a crime involved Detroit's underbelly of brokered sex, it was inevitable that big names turned up…politicians and cops included.

"All I can say—" the older man said under his breath "—is that bitch better watch her back."

The venom in his tone caught Remy off guard and he wanted to ask which woman was the bitch—the defendant or her attorney—when the courtroom doors burst open and two reporters barreled out. Remy got up and slipped out, too.

He'd seen enough. If Charlie Street could help him, he didn't give a flying fuck if *she* was Jack the Ripper.

Hitch followed on Remy's heels and headed toward the exit, tossing out over his shoulder, "Sorry about Adam, man. He was a damn good cop."

Remy's gut twisted. *Still is.*

He gritted his teeth against a sudden, fierce urge to punch something.

He fucking still is.

Behind him, the courtroom doors banged open, gain, and he stepped aside as the first wave of spectators poured out. Christ, everyone from the governor's office on down had a stake in this high-octane case. Once the attorney was outside, the gang of reporters and paps playing bumper bodies on the courthouse steps would swarm her like she was Lady Gaga. There'd be no way in hell he could talk to her, privately or otherwise.

As the people filtered out, he spotted the attorney behind a bailiff redirecting her to the room between the courtroom and the judges' chambers. The room had two doors, and he was guessing she'd go out the other side to avoid the media circus.

He separated himself from the remaining court groupies and headed to the next hallway, reaching the exit just as the attorney was coming out, ass first, briefcase in one hand and a stack of files in the other.

As she pulled the door shut, he said, "Miss Street, can I talk to you for a moment?"

She froze, her back ramrod stiff. "You just did," she said, still with her back to him. "If you're a reporter—no comment. If you want a consult—" she turned…ice-blue eyes raked over him "—make an appointment."

Crushing the armful of files against her chest, she pivoted, and then made a beeline down the hall.

He bit back a nasty retort and, after a pause, started after her.

Just as he got close enough to say something, a hulking black dude in a too-tight gray suit appeared at her side, as if from nowhere. Remy stopped in his tracks.

The attorney, still walking, took the guy's arm and they headed toward the side exit together.

Remy planted his feet apart, crossed his arms and, hot blood still sizzling in his veins, watched them disappear around the corner.

Yeah. Now he knew which woman was the bitch.

You sure you're okay?" Dempsey asked as they reached Charlie's car.

"I'm perfect. Couldn't be better." She pasted on a smile, glad the former boxing champ who sparred with students at her brother's neighborhood gym had volunteered to act as her "bodyguard" during the trial.

She did a quick scan of the parking area, pulled the keys from her jacket pocket, and pressed the unlock button on the fob.

Dempsey shot her a skeptical look. "If you say so." The big man opened the car door for her.

"Just another reporter." She dropped her files and messenger bag on the floor in the back, slid into the driver's seat, and kicked off her heels. Wearing new shoes when she had to stand for hours had been a bad pre-coffee decision, and not her first of the day.

She buckled her seatbelt, started the car, and waited for Dempsey to come around on the passenger side. The police had determined the shooting three months ago to be random, a stray bullet, probably gang related, given the neighborhood. And the threat letter she'd received was likely another crank.

She was getting used to those. Most of the cases she worked on made someone unhappy. When her brother first suggested she get protection for the Devonshire trial, she'd balked at the idea. Even if she'd been the target three months ago, having a bodyguard wasn't going to stop a bullet.

But Landon had made a convincing argument that being seen with some well-respected muscle during the trial wouldn't hurt. She couldn't deny she felt more secure with a little heavy duty testosterone at her side, if only to deflect the paparazzi and court creeps.

Like the guy who'd been lurking outside the judges' chambers. If Dempsey hadn't shown up, the jerk would've dogged her, for sure.

Once Dempsey crammed himself inside her Focus, she pulled out and headed to the lot where he'd parked his vehicle. Her stomach growled, reminding her that food was sometimes a necessity.

"How long before the trial is over?"

"Why? You tired of being my escort?"

The big man chuckled. "Easiest job ever. But I got another gig pretty soon, so I was just wonderin'."

"Closing arguments are coming up. After that, there's just the verdict. If you have something else to do, go ahead. It's been a long trial, and I'm sure you have more exciting things to do than babysit me." She glanced over. Smiled at Dempsey.

She hadn't taken on a murder trial since she'd been a public defender five years ago. Aside from her pro bono cases, most of the work done by her team at Street Law was investigative.

She tipped her head to the side and rubbed the back of her neck. Damn, she was tired. Trials were exhausting, and she couldn't wait to be finished. But that wasn't going to happen until she'd done everything possible to convince the jury her client was innocent.

Still, given Lucy's profession, it was a tough sell. Not that it mattered. Not when someone's life was hanging in the balance. She'd do whatever she had to do to see an innocent person acquitted.

"You need me for that meeting tonight?" Dempsey asked as she pulled her car in next to his.

"No. I'm good." She forced another smile. "As much as I like your company, Demps, people with secrets don't feel much like talking when there's an audience."

He opened the door and got out. "Yeah, but you don't know—"

"There'll be enough people in the restaurant to intervene if the guy's not on the level."

He gave her a three-finger salute and closed the door.

Tonight would probably be another bust anyway. She hadn't uncovered anything new on her father's case in years and had pretty much quit the search. But she couldn't take a pass on any scrap of information that might help prove her father's innocence. No matter how nervous she was about it.

The evidence was out there, but like Jimmy Hoffa's body, it was just too deeply buried to find.

She drew her bottom lip between her teeth. Twenty-five years ago today. But somehow…someday…she would find who framed her father and orchestrated his murder in prison.

Justice would prevail. One way or another.

On the road, again, she turned on the radio, glad to be going home. There was just enough time for a nap before the meeting.

Humming along with J-Lo, she clicked on her blinker, moved over a lane, then checked the rearview mirror for the upcoming turn onto Michigan Avenue. Seeing a black car closer than she liked, she sped ahead a little to put space between them. But the idiot sped up, too, until he was on her bumper again.

Jerk. In the mirror she could see the person was big. A man. But between the dusky light and his lowered visor, she couldn't see his face. She pumped her brake to warn him to back off. Instead, he accelerated and rammed her bumper. Her head slammed forward and back.

Her pulse skyrocketed. What the…? She tightened her grip on the wheel, accelerated to pass a car on her right, then slid over a lane to get rid of the maniac. But she saw his vehicle doing the same…and then he was right behind her, again. And closing in, as if to ram her.

What the hell was he doing?

She reached for her phone. *Shit*. It was in her bag in the back, and she couldn't take her eyes off the road to get it. Someone needed to report this idiot. She pumped her brakes again and, this time, he veered sharply left and merged into the next lane. A quick sense of relief swept through her. Good. Stay there, asshole.

But just as she thought it, he sped up next to her, pacing her car at the same speed.

Her heart racing, she gritted her teeth and focused on the road. *Don't look*. That's what he wants. Classic case of road rage. She knew the psychology. He wanted to intimidate her. Scare her. If she flipped him off or called him a name, it would only exacerbate the situation, and it could get even more dangerous.

Tires squealed and she saw his car swerve over. The grating crunch of metal against metal pierced her ears, jolted her vehicle sideways into the path of a semi bearing down on her right. She yanked the wheel left. Her car twisted sideways. She turned into the curve, blood pounding in her ears as she got the car under control.

Geezus. Crazy. The guy was totally freaking crazy.

Okay...okay...deep breath, Charlie. Stay calm. She couldn't turn off the road and have him follow her home, and she didn't dare stop or who knew what he'd do. She slowed. Maybe he'd get tired of not getting the response he wanted and disappear.

He slowed, too.

Oh, God! He wasn't going to quit.

Her spirits leapt when she spied two police vehicles at a gas station just ahead. Barely slowing, she made a quick right into the driveway and, as she did, she turned to look at the man harassing her.

Had to. She needed to know if he was just some angry dickhead taking out his aggressions behind the wheel...or someone who might actually want to harm her.

Like someone who feared exposure at the Lucy Devonshire trial.

Or the man who'd been waiting for her outside the courtroom.

To read more of DETROIT RULES,
go to Amazon.com or visit my website.

LindaStyle.com

A Note from the Author

Dear Reader,

Thank you for being a reader and sharing your love of reading by purchasing my stories. I hope you enjoyed STREET, book one in my Street Law series, and if so, then you're sure to like DETROIT RULES, book two in the series. In book two, Charlie has come a long way. I like the person she's become, and I hope she'll succeed in her quest for justice.

I also hope that you'll consider leaving a review or rating for STREET on Amazon and Goodreads, or wherever you like to hang out and chat about books. If you haven't read my other books, I hope you'll want to pick them up and spend more time with characters I love and who have become like part of my family while writing their stories. I love to hear from readers and also connect on social media. If you'd like to chat and keep updated on future releases, please join me on:
Facebook: @LindaStyle
Twitter: @LindaStyle
I'm also on Instagram, so please stop by and join the fun.

If you'd like to sign up for my newsletter and be the first to learn about book sales and freebies, you can do so on my Linda Style Amazon page and on my website.

LindaStyle.com

Best wishes and Happy Reading,

Linda

Also by Linda Style

Fiction from LMS Press
Copyright © Linda Fensand Syle

Her Sister's Secret, 2nd edition
Cowboys Don't Dance

SECRETS OF SPIRIT CREEK series: romance
Remember Me, Book 1
Trust Me, Book 2
Rescue Me, Book 3

L.A.P.D. SPECIAL INVESTIGATIONS series: romantic suspense

The Forgotten, Book 1
The Deceived, Book 2
The Taken, Book 3
The Silent, Book 4
The Missing, Book 5

STREET LAW series: crime thriller
Street, Book 1
Detroit Rules, Book 2
Detroit Hustle, Book 3 (Coming Soon)

Fiction: Backlist from Harlequin Enterprises Ltd
Copyright © Linda Fendsand Style

Her Sister's Secret
Daddy in the House
Slow Dance with a Cowboy
The Man in the Photograph
What Madeline Wants

The Witness
His Case, Her Child
And Justice for All
Husband and Wife Reunion
Going for Broke
The Man from Texas
The Mistake She Made
The Promise He Made
A Soldier's Secret
Protecting the Witness

Non-Fiction:

BOOTCAMP FOR NOVELISTS BEYOND THE FIRST DRAFT: Writing Techniques of the Pros
In digital and in print.

By Linda Style Copyright © 2013, LMS Press, Gilbert, AZ 85234. (403 pages)

BOOTCAMP FOR NOVELISTS BEYOND THE FIRST DRAFT Parts I, II, and III
Digital Only

Linda's books are available on her website, on Amazon, and other bookstore outlets.

LindaStyle.com

About the Author

LINDA STYLE is an Award-Winning, National Bestselling author with over a million copies sold in thirteen different countries. With an education in behavioral science and in journalism, Linda has worked in a number of jobs, from social services to Director of a state mental health program, to magazine editor. She's also worked as a writing instructor at Bootcamp for Novelists, an online writing school she co-founded in 2004, but as rewarding as all that all was, she says nothing compares with writing her stories of suspense, romance, and intrigue. Her books—often described as emotional, fast-paced stories that keep you riveted to the page—have won several awards, including the prestigious Daphne du Maurier Award of Excellence, the Orange Rose award for Best Book of the Year, and the HOLT Award of Merit.

When not writing, Linda loves to travel, a passion that has taken her all over the world and allows her to indulge in her other passion…photography. A Minnesota native, she now lives with her family in Arizona, where she likes to play tennis and hike in the mountains—the best place in the world to think up more stories. She invites you to stop by her website.

LindaStyle.com